'Why don't yo[...]
inside you, Ed[...]

'Why do you want [...]

'Don't answer a question with a question.'

'I always do that when I don't want to answer a question with an answer.'

Jack thought about that for a moment. 'No one is more surprised than I am, but I actually understood that.' He looked into her eyes. 'So let me answer for you. You don't want me looking into your dark corners.'

Dear Reader

This month finds us once again well and truly into winter—season of snow, celebration and new beginnings. And whatever the weather, you can rely on Mills & Boon to bring you sixteen magical new romances to help keep out the cold! We've found you a great selection of stories from all over the world—so let us take you in your mid-winter reading to a Winter Wonderland of love, excitement, and above all, romance!

The Editor

Brittany Young lives and writes in Racine, Wisconsin. She has travelled to most of the countries that serve as the settings for her romances and finds the research into the language, customs, history and literature of these countries among the most demanding and rewarding aspects of her writing.

A MAN CALLED TRAVERS

BY

BRITTANY YOUNG

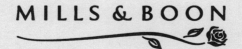

MILLS & BOON

MILLS & BOON LIMITED
ETON HOUSE, 18-24 PARADISE ROAD
RICHMOND, SURREY TW9 1SR

Original edition published in 1989
by Silhouette Romances

First published in Great Britain 1994
by Mills & Boon Limited

© Brittany Young 1989

Australian copyright 1994
Philippine copyright 1994
This edition 1994

ISBN 0 263 78362 6

Set in Times Roman 10 on 12¼ pt.
01-9401-42217 C

Made and printed in Great Britain

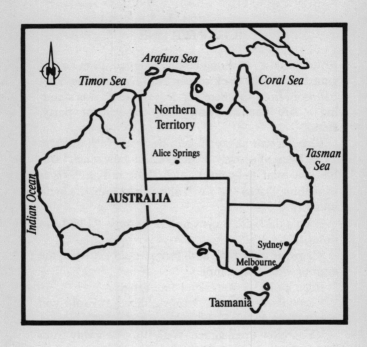

CHAPTER ONE

EDEN SLOANE, her long blonde hair caught in an elegant twist at the back of her head, crossed the hotel ballroom floor to where her dearest friend was standing. "Are you enjoying your engagement party, Beth?"

Beth affectionately linked her arm with Eden's. "Oh, Eden, it's lovely. I can't believe how much trouble you went to—and at such short notice. This is something David and I will always remember. Thank you."

Eden's dark green eyes smiled warmly. "I had fun doing it."

"Now, if only Jack and Terry would get here, the evening would be complete."

Eden looked at her friend enquiringly.

"David's brothers," Beth explained. "I told you about them, didn't I?"

"Yes. Now I remember. Well, it's a long way from Australia. Perhaps their flight was delayed."

"I suppose." There was a stir near the door and Beth's face suddenly lit up. "They made it! There's Jack."

Eden looked across the room and saw a tall—very tall—man impeccably dressed in a dinner-jacket and looking as comfortable as though he wore one every day. His hair was dark, short at the sides and well past his collar in the back. Eden didn't normally like hair that long on men, but on him it looked exactly right. She could tell even from this distance that his eyes were blue and thickly lashed. "Why, Beth, he's gorgeous!" Eden said in undisguised surprise.

Beth flashed her friend an amused look. "Of course he is. What were you expecting?"

"Oh, I don't know. The outback version of Crocodile Dundee. Certainly not Mel Gibson in a tuxedo."

This time Beth laughed. "Believe it or not, civilisation has made it to the outback, Eden."

"Apparently."

"Come on," Beth said as she took Eden's hand and led her across the room. "I'll introduce you."

Jack was standing there, gazing around the room. He turned when Beth placed her hand on his arm and smiled down at her. "Jack," she said with a beaming smile, "I'm glad you could make it."

His strong arms enveloped her in a hug. "I wouldn't have missed it for the world. Where's Dave?"

"Mingling, like a good boy." She turned to Eden. "Jack Travers," she said, formally introducing them, "I'd like you to meet my dearest friend in the world, and our hostess, Eden Sloane."

Jack saw a woman somewhere in her mid-twenties, her blonde hair pulled severely back, emphasising her pale, perfectly oval face. Her eyes were large and emerald-coloured, her nose perfectly proportioned to her face, and her mouth, lightly tinted, was full and beautifully etched. She was like a Dresden doll, perfect in every detail, delicate, aloof—and utterly untouchable. Jack inclined his dark head. ''G'day, Miss Sloane.''

''Please,'' she said as she extended her hand, ''call me Eden.''

Beth looked beyond his shoulder. ''Where's Terry?''

Jack released Eden's hand and also turned to look. ''I don't know, Beth. He was right behind me a minute ago.''

Beth clicked her tongue. ''Honestly, that man. Knowing Terry, he probably got waylaid by a pretty face. I'd better find him or he may never make it to the party.''

As Beth walked away, Jack turned his attention to Eden. ''I understand that you're coming to Australia next week for the wedding,'' he said politely.

''Yes, I am.''

''Have you ever been there before?''

''No.''

Jack's blue gaze took in her cool sophistication. ''Ever wanted to go there?'' he asked, knowing the answer.

''I can't honestly say that I have.''

''Too rustic?'' he guessed.

''Something like that. I'm a city girl.''

''We have cities in Australia.''

''Not the part of Australia that you're from.''

''We have something better there.''

''What's that?''

"Wide open space where you can go for miles without coming across another human being."

"But I like human beings."

"Eden, darling, there you are!" A man with wavy light brown hair walked over to her and gave her a chaste kiss on the cheek but otherwise didn't touch her. "I'm sorry I'm so late, but I just got back into town a few hours ago and then got held up at the office. How's the party going?"

"Beautifully." She looked at the Australian. "Jack Travers, meet Richard Austen III. Richard, this is David Travers's brother, Jack."

Jack shook Richard's extended hand, then Richard lightly but possessively rested his hand on Eden's shoulder. "Are you the one with the cattle ranch?"

Jack looked at Richard's hand. "Right."

"We're looking forward to seeing your place. David's told us a lot about it."

His eyes moved to Eden. "You're coming together?"

Uncharacteristically, Eden found herself at a loss for words, and it was left to Richard to answer. "We need to get in a little ceremonial practice." He smiled at Eden as he lightly squeezed her shoulder. "Our wedding is next."

Jack looked from one to the other, his eyes coming back to Eden. "Congratulations."

"Thank you." Richard was oblivious to the undercurrents.

Another man suddenly appeared. He was tall, like Jack, and deeply tanned. "G'day," he said, eyeing Eden appreciatively. "Who's the tart?"

Eden's eyes widened in surprise, but it was Richard whose shocked voice dropped into the lower registers. "I beg your pardon?"

"Oh, don't go crook on me, mate. All women are called tarts where I come from. Does she belong to you?"

After her initial shock Eden found her voice. "I don't *belong* to anyone."

"Too right!" He grabbed her and planted a big kiss on her unsuspecting mouth. "What's your name, beautiful?" he asked as he released her.

"Eden Sloane," she said evenly, "and if you ever do anything like that to me again without my permission, you'll be walking with a permanent limp."

Terry's grin grew wider. "No worries. I meant no offence." He turned his attention to Richard. "And who's this standing next to you staring at me like a stunned mullet?"

The description was so perfect that it was all Eden could do to keep from laughing out loud. She settled for clearing her throat. "This is Richard Austen."

"The Third," added Richard with dignity as he reluctantly extended his hand.

"Nice to meet you, Dickie."

Eden finally figured out what was going on and turned eyes brimming with laughter to Terry. "Now that you've tweaked our noses, can you speak in English?"

12   A MAN CALLED TRAVERS

His lightning smile flashed. "You're quick."

"Not quick enough, apparently."

"You'll do, Eden Sloane. You'll do just fine."

"Will someone tell me what's going on?" Richard asked impatiently.

"We're just having a bit of fun, Dickie," Terry said as he gave Richard a friendly slap on the back. "Don't be so serious. Life's too short."

Beth walked over to Richard at that moment and slipped her arm through his. "Good. I'm glad to see you've all found each other. Richard," she said more quietly, "there's a man named Goodspeed who's looking for you."

"Where is he?"

"By the bar. At least, that's where he was the last time I saw him."

"Thank you." He looked at Eden with an apologetic smile. "I'll be right back, darling."

"I'm coming with you," Beth said as she followed him. "David's over there."

Terry suddenly touched Eden's arm. "Who's that?"

Her eyes followed the direction of his inclined head. "The redhead?"

"The one with the incredible..." He held both hands in front of his chest in an unmistakable gesture but he caught himself when he remembered who he was talking to. "Yeah, the one with the incredible red hair."

It was impossible not to like Terry Travers. "Catherine Moreland."

"Who's that she's with? Husband?"

"She's divorced. He's just her date."

Terry reached up and straightened his bow tie, then pulled back his shoulders. "Excuse me, all, but my hormones are calling and Catherine is the name on their lips."

Once again, Eden found herself awkwardly alone with Jack Travers. She turned to him with the polite smile of a perfect hostess. "Are you hungry? There's lots of food and it's all delicious."

Blue eyes moved over her with a slow thoroughness that missed nothing until they returned to her own gaze. "I'm not really hungry right now. Excuse me, Eden."

She watched in surprise as Jack walked away from her.

"Eden?" Beth said. "You're a million miles away."

"I think it's safe to say there's someone here who wishes I were."

"Who? What are you talking about?"

"Never mind." Eden smiled at her friend as she listened to the strains of a waltz played by the twelve-piece orchestra she'd hired. "I feel like dancing. Do you know where Richard is?"

"Near the bar talking business, as usual."

Eden's gaze involuntarily returned to the Australian who was standing so that his profile was in her line of vision. Jack suddenly turned his head and his eyes went straight to hers. He didn't smile. He just looked. Then he turned away.

Eden felt an uncharacteristic jolt, which she quickly pushed aside. "I think I'll interrupt." She crossed the room, stopping here and there to chat with the guests, unaware of a pair of intense blue eyes tracking her.

When Eden got to Richard, he smiled down at her as he took her aside. "I'm sorry," he apologised. "I know this always seems to happen at parties, but I have to leave."

Eden's heart sank. She didn't know why it was so important to her that he stay, but it was. "Business?"

"I'm afraid so."

"Can't it wait until tomorrow?"

"I'm sorry, darling, but no."

She tried to smile as though it didn't matter. "Oh, well. Perhaps you can return later. I'll save a dance for you."

"It's a nice thought but doubtful. I'll call you to-morrow." He kissed her forehead.

"All right," she said quietly.

He started to walk away.

"Richard?"

He turned back with a smile that hinted of impatience. "Yes?"

"Kiss me."

"I just did."

"I don't mean a peck on the forehead. I mean a real kiss."

Richard looked around to see if their conversation were being eavesdropped upon. "Eden," he said, moving closer and lowering his voice, "there are people watching."

"So?"

"I have no intention of making a public spectacle of either myself or you." A frown creased his forehead. "What's wrong with you?"

"I don't know," she said honestly. "Sorry."

He looked at her for a moment longer. "Well, as I said, I'll call you tomorrow. Goodnight."

Her eyes followed Richard's receding back until he disappeared from sight. She turned with a sigh, only to find Jack Travers standing about ten feet away, a drink in his hand, talking with an attractive woman. The woman apparently said something amusing because his eyes crinkled appealingly at the corners.

"Personally, I think he should have kissed you," a heavily accented voice said next to her ear. "I certainly wouldn't have passed up an offer like that."

Eden turned her head slightly and smiled at Terry, but not without a little embarrassment. "I can't imagine you turning down an offer of any sort. How did you get along with the fair Catherine?"

"I think she was attracted, but she has her eye on larger game than a station hand from the Territory who doesn't have a brass razoo to his name."

"Are you sure it wasn't your approach?"

"What's wrong with my approach?"

"Absolutely nothing if one happens to be a woman who enjoys being hit over the head and dragged off to a cave."

Terry grinned and his teeth flashed white in his dark face. "Subtlety never has been one of my strong points."

Eden grinned back at him. "No!"

He grabbed her hand suddenly. "Come on, gorgeous. Let's have a go at the dance floor."

As soon as they were away from the majority of the people, he turned her into his arms and began swaying to the music. Eden looked at him in surprise. "You're not bad."

"Did you think I was going to ruin those new shoes of yours?"

"I was more concerned with the feet inside the shoes."

Terry smiled down at her. "Eden Sloane, I like you."

"You sound surprised."

"I am. At first I thought you were a bit too sophisticated for my taste, but you kind of grow on a man."

"Thank you—I think."

"You're quite welcome." His smile grew. "And if you don't mind a little personal advice, dump Richard. He's not for you." He suddenly spotted Jack and took his hand from Eden's waist so he could grab his brother's arm. "Hey, Jack, let me have a turn with our sister-to-be. You take a spin with Eden, here."

Eden stiffened as she found herself standing in the middle of the dance floor, deserted by Terry and looking into the blue eyes of Jack Travers. "Actually," she said with cool politeness bordering on cold, "I should be mingling with the guests. Excuse me."

As she began to walk around him, Jack put a strong hand at her slender waist, his eyes never leaving hers. "Dance with me, Eden."

"I . . ."

"I'm a guest."

She hesitated only a moment before moving into his arms. The fingers of her right hand meshed intimately with his as the warm hand at her waist pulled her body close. Close, yet not touching his. She tried to think about something other than the fact of his nearness, but it was impossible. She couldn't take a breath without inhaling the clean scent of him. Eden pressed her free hand lightly against his solid chest and looked up at him as their bodies swayed rhythmically. She studied his chin, fascinated by the faint indentation there. Her gaze moved to his chiselled mouth and then to the intense eyes that were examining her with just as much care.

Never in her life had Eden been this aware of another human being. Her breath literally caught in her throat every time his body brushed against hers. Suddenly she just stopped dancing and stepped back from him, filled with an almost panicked need to get away. "Excuse me. I really have to go." She backed away from him a few more steps and bumped into another couple. She turned with a sharp breath. "I'm so sorry. Excuse me." Then she walked off the dance floor as quickly as dignity would allow.

"Have you ever lost your touch," Terry told his brother as he danced by with Beth.

But Jack wasn't listening. His eyes were still on the woman doing her best to get away from him.

*   *   *

It was nearly one in the morning when the last of the guests said goodbye and left. Eden, who was standing at the entrance to the ballroom with Beth and David, turned to her friend with a tired smile. "I know I shouldn't say this about my own party, but I had a great time."

David, looking very much like his blond brother, Terry, reached over and squeezed Eden's hand. "So did Beth and I. Thank you."

Terry suddenly came racing past them. "Excuse me, all, but I have a date."

"Do you have any idea what time it is?" Beth asked.

"A very precise idea."

"Catherine?" Eden guessed.

"The one and only," he told her with a grin.

"How did you manage it?"

"Personally, I think someone told her about Jack and she got the two of us confused, but," he shrugged, "who am I to quibble with fate?" He winked at Eden and then leaned over and kissed her on the cheek. "Goodbye, gorgeous. See you in Australia."

"Is he always like that?" Eden asked David with a smile as Terry rapidly disappeared from sight.

"Always. He loves women. Of course, it also helps that he's a little crazy."

Still smiling, Eden crossed the room to where the small orchestra was packing up. She shook hands with all of them as she thanked them and then did the same with the bartenders and waiters who were still cleaning up.

Jack's deep, slightly gravelly voice came from behind her. "Beth said that this was yours."

Eden turned to find him holding her coat. "It is, thank you."

Jack held it for her while she slipped her arms into the silk-lined sleeves. When his hands smoothed the fabric over her shoulders in a perfectly normal gesture, Eden closed her eyes. This was ridiculous. He was just an ordinary man. Taking a deep breath, she turned to him with a cool smile that hid the warmth inside her. "Thank you, again." She extended her hand. "I hope you have a safe trip home."

Jack took her hand and held it for a moment. Then he let it go.

Beth, her arm looped through David's, walked towards them. "Is your driver coming to pick you up, Eden?"

"No. I knew I'd be late, so I gave him the night off."

"How are you getting home?"

"Taxi."

"You most certainly are not," Beth told her. "We're going with Jack. I'm sure he wouldn't mind dropping you off—would you, Jack?" she asked, turning to the Australian.

Eden didn't want to get in a car with him. "Beth, I . . ."

But Jack was ahead of her. "Of course I wouldn't mind."

"That's settled then. Let's go."

It would have looked odd if she'd protested, so Eden followed them out of the ballroom and through the nearly deserted lobby to the glass doors that led outside.

"I'll go for the car and bring it around. You three wait here," Jack told them as he raised the collar of his coat against the cold and left.

While they waited, David looked at Eden and frowned. "Are you all right?"

"Of course. Why do you ask?"

"I don't really know. You seem a bit edgy."

She smiled unconvincingly. "I always get nervous when I give a party. Hostess jitters."

She could see by his expression that David thought she'd seemed fine earlier, but he didn't say that.

At last Jack pulled into the hotel's circular driveway. David opened the front passenger door for Eden and then slid into the back seat with Beth.

"Where do you live, Eden?" Jack asked.

She looked straight through the windscreen. "About two miles from here. Drive to the next traffic light and turn left."

An uncomfortable silence fell between them.

"How are things at the station?" David asked as his brother put the car into gear and moved into the light flow of traffic.

"Dry."

"And the stock?"

"Getting thirstier and thinner."

"Are you going to try to move them closer to water?"

"Not unless I have to. That kind of trip could decimate the herd."

"Can't you bring the water to them?" Eden asked.

Jack looked at her, apparently surprised that she was interested enough to ask a question. "For reasons I won't bore you with here, it's not a solution."

Eden went back to gazing through the windscreen. "Turn right at the next corner," she said quietly.

Jack made the turn and then glanced at her again. Eden felt his eyes on her profile, but she continued to look straight ahead. "Turn left."

He did.

"That's my building," she said as she pointed to one halfway down the block.

Jack parked nearby, got out, then walked around the car and opened the door for her. "I'll be right back," he told David and Beth, then closed the door and walked into the building with Eden. She turned to him when they got to the lift. "I appreciate your bringing me home, but there's no need for you to go upstairs. The building has strict security, so I doubt that anyone will mug me between the lobby and my floor."

"I don't know, Eden. The guard let me in without a second look, didn't he?"

Eden looked at him in surprise. Humour? For the first time since she'd met him, a genuine smile touched her mouth, and the man felt his heart catch at the beauty of it. "That's true. Maybe you'd better go up with me after all."

Just then the lift arrived and the two of them got on. Neither said anything on the ride to the top floor, nor did they say anything as they walked down the hall to her apartment. Eden took her keys from her purse and opened the door, then looked at Jack. "Thank you for driving me home."

"You're welcome." His eyes roamed over her face. "Have you ever heard the saying that 'you can run but you can't hide'?"

"Yes." She looked at him in confusion. "Why?"

"Oh, no reason. It's just something that popped into my mind. Goodnight, Eden."

Eden's gaze followed his receding back. He was leaving. She could relax.

Jack took the lift to the first floor and walked through the lobby out to the car. When he was behind the steering wheel, he sat there, still and silent.

"Jack?" David leaned forward and touched his brother's shoulder. "What's wrong?"

He shook his head. "Nothing. Where's my hotel?"

"North," Beth said, pointing in the general direction.

Jack took the keys out of the ignition and tossed them over his shoulder to David. "You two take the car. I feel like walking."

"But it's probably fifteen miles from here!"

"Good." He got out, closed the door and had started off before either David or Beth could think of anything else to say. They looked at each other, shrugged and climbed into the front seat.

CHAPTER TWO

A WEEK later, as the jet Eden was on prepared to land in Sydney, a flight attendant approached her. "Are you Miss Sloane?"

She looked up from fastening her seat belt. "Yes."

"I have a message for you from someone named Beth. As soon as we land, you're to go directly to the private terminal where there will be a plane waiting to take you to your final destination."

"Did she say who the pilot was going to be?"

"I'm afraid not."

"Thank you." Eden leaned back in her seat and stared out the window at the cloudless bright blue sky, knowing instinctively that Jack Travers was going to be the pilot. "Oh, Richard," she sighed to herself, "why couldn't you have just left work long enough to come to the wedding with me?"

Eden leaned her head against the rim of the window and watched as the plane dropped lower over the foaming surf of Sydney's shores, circling for almost twenty minutes before finally landing. Warm air surrounded her as soon as she stepped from the plane on to the tarmac—a delightful change from the frigid temperatures she'd left behind in New York. She collected her luggage and quickly cleared customs, then started the long walk through the busy airport to the private terminal.

No sooner had she got there than she heard herself being paged. Walking over to a courtesy phone, she set her luggage down and picked up the receiver. "This is Eden Sloane."

"So, you finally made it to Australia."

The voice hadn't come from the phone. It had come from behind her. Eden hesitated just a moment before hanging up the receiver and turning to face Jack Travers. "Hello."

"G'day, Eden. Where's your Richard?"

"He couldn't come after all."

"I see. That's too bad." Jack took her suitcases and started walking down the concourse with long strides. Eden had to run a few steps to catch up with him. "Why are you in such a hurry?" she asked breathlessly when she finally caught up and managed to match her stride to his.

"There's work to be done, and I don't have any more time to waste standing around an airport." He didn't sound annoyed. Just matter-of-fact.

"Perhaps you should have sent someone else."

"Ah, but that would be a sign of a bad host, wouldn't it?"

She was determined not to take offence. "How far away is your home?"

"Fifteen hundred miles, give or take a few hundred."

Eden stopped walking. "You flew all that way just to pick me up?"

Jack stopped also and turned to look at her. "I couldn't very well leave you to fend for yourself."

"I'm very good at fending for myself."

Jack's eyes met her steady green gaze. "I bet you are at that. Why didn't you come last week when everyone else did?"

"Some business matters came up and delayed Richard. I stayed in New York, hoping that his calendar would clear up so that we'd be able to come together."

"Is he flying in later?"

"It doesn't look like it." There was something about Jack Travers that made Eden feel she needed to explain. "You see, his work is important. With the way things are in the stockmarket right now, people who rely on his advice could lose a lot of money if he were to simply leave."

"I see."

"His customers would be disappointed in him."

"As opposed to just you," Jack said coolly.

Eden looked at him curiously. He sounded annoyed on her behalf. "Something like that. Not that it's really any of your business."

"True." Jack turned and started walking again. This time Eden didn't try to catch up but followed him through the rest of the concourse and out the sliding glass doors to the tarmac and the waiting red and white propeller plane. Jack stowed her luggage on board, then turned to Eden a little impatiently. "Come on."

As she moved towards him, Jack put his hands at her waist and lifted her on to the plane, then walked around to the other side.

Eden strapped herself in and watched Jack as he readied things for takeoff and spoke into the small microphone attached to his headset.

He glanced at her. "Ready?"

"Yes."

He slowly taxied the little plane down the runway to wait in line with everyone else. Eden watched the planes take off ahead of them one by one until it was finally their turn. Jack spoke into the headset again, waited for some instructions, then nosed the plane around on to the runway and gunned it.

Within seconds they were in the air, soaring over the airport in a great arc. The ocean waves that lapped against Sydney's shores came into view, and as they climbed higher there were mountains. Beautiful, age-worn, ancient mountains that strung along for as far as the eye could see.

"Those are the Blue Mountains," Jack explained. "They're part of the Dividing Range."

Eden could see why they were called *Blue*. That was exactly the colour of the air around them.

"That haze," Jack told her, as though sensing her thoughts, "is caused by droplets of eucalyptus oil shining in the atmosphere." He veered the plane slightly to the right and flew low over the deep gorges so she could see the high silvery waterfalls as they fell foaming into shady pools below. "Take a good look. Those are the last hills you'll be seeing for a long time."

Even as he spoke the words, the slopes gently leveled out to merge with the inland plain, neatly broken up by paddocks with scattered flocks of sheep. The carpet of green grass was occasionally interrupted by golden geometric patches where wheat grew. Corrugated tin roofs glinted in the sunlight.

Eden sat silent, her gaze riveted on the scene unfolding below as the counterpane of paddocks gradually gave way over the next hour to a seemingly endless expanse of gray-green shrubs and then changed yet again as the colours of the increasingly flat earth altered almost imperceptibly from khaki and green to an arid, inflamed red. There were places where the earth was fissured by dry riverbeds that reached out like thin, arthritic fingers. Heat rose from the barren ground in waves, distorting the view.

"Quite a sight, don't you think?"

Eden turned and met Jack's gaze. "It's remarkable," she told him honestly. "I don't think I've ever seen land that goes from one extreme to another in such a short distance."

"What you see now is pretty much the way things will stay for the rest of the trip."

"Your land looks like this?" she asked in surprise as she looked out at the dry, chapped earth.

"More or less."

"How do you raise cattle?"

"Over the years I've put a lot of time and money into locating underground water reservoirs on the station. They're few and far between, but so far they're providing enough for the cattle to drink and to irrigate some of the pastures."

"So far?" She turned her eyes to his profile and was surprised to see the concern that was etched at the corner of his mouth and in the groove in his cheek.

"It's been nearly fourteen months since we've had any rain. Everything's got to dry up sooner or later if there's nothing to replenish it."

"What happens if the water runs out?"

He shook his head. "Let's just hope it doesn't come to that."

After that they both fell silent. Eden leaned back in her seat and stared out the window. Jack was different from anyone she'd ever met, and she honestly didn't know how to read him. She only knew that he made her uncomfortable. There were times when she felt that his blue eyes could see right through her.

The quiet hours sped by. Eden kept trying to get lost in her thoughts, but her attention always came back to the Australian.

When the plane began a sudden descent, Eden, who was never thrilled about travelling on large planes, never mind small ones, sat up straight and looked nervously out of the window. "What's happening? Are we at your station?"

Jack looked at her in surprise. It was the first indication he'd had that she was tense. "Relax. We're just refuelling." Moments later he landed smoothly at a small airstrip and taxied over to the only building on the property. A man walked towards them, wiping greasy hands on a red and white chequered rag. Jack unfastened his seat belt and opened his door. "There's no need for you to get out. We're only going to be here a few minutes."

Eden watched him climb down and sat quietly for a while, but it was boring and she wanted to stretch her legs, so she opened her own door and jumped to the ground.

She literally gasped as the heat rose up from the concrete and hit her in the face. It was like walking into a blast furnace. Almost immediately a fine film of perspiration broke out on her forehead. She walked around the plane, her high heels clicking on the pavement, to where Jack stood speaking with the man doing the refuelling.

He stopped in midsentence to look at her. "You were better off staying in the plane, Eden."

"I just wanted to walk around. It seems as if I've spent the last couple of days doing nothing but sitting."

"Suit yourself, but you're not used to the heat."

"I'm very adaptable."

Jack lifted a sceptical brow as he looked at her porcelain skin. She was already flushed. "Right."

Eden smiled at him, charming the man despite himself. "Watch it. I might surprise you."

A slow smile curved his mouth in response. "And then again, you might be the one who's surprised."

Turning away from her, he resumed his conversation with the man beside him.

Feeling dismissed, Eden wandered away from the plane. Squinting against the bright sun, she climbed a small hill and stood under a sun-dwarfed tree that offered little in the way of shade. There wasn't much to see. Just scattered trees like the one she was under, scrub and scorched red earth.

Jack came up the hill and stood beside her. "You shouldn't be out in the sun with that skin of yours."

Once again she found herself uncomfortably aware of the man. What was it about him that made her react that way? "Considering where we are, that's going to be rather difficult."

"As soon as we get to the station, I'll suit you up with proper clothes and a hat."

Her eyes met his. "That's nice of you."

"You sound surprised."

"No comment." Eden looked into the distance again. "Do people really live out there?"

"They do."

"Why?" She honestly couldn't imagine why people would voluntarily subject themselves to it.

"Because they love it. You'll begin to understand that emotion when you've been here for a few days."

"Perhaps."

He held out his hand to help her down the hill. "Come on. We have to get going."

Eden looked at him a moment before placing her hand in his. She managed to get down without stumbling by digging her heels into the packed dirt. Jack released her hand as soon as they were on level ground, touching her again only to help her onto the plane. A few minutes later they were racing down the runway once more and lifting into the air.

He glanced over at Eden as soon as the plane had levelled off. "You look tired."

"Thank you," she said drily.

"It wasn't meant as a criticism, just an observation. Did you manage to get any sleep on the flight from the States?"

"I can't sleep on planes."

"Afraid you're going to miss the crash?"

A smile curved her mouth. He was very observant. "Something like that."

"Then it won't do any good for me to suggest you try to rest for the remainder of the flight. We have at least three more hours in the air."

"I'm content to just sit quietly."

"Actually, there's a trick to sleeping on any plane."

"Knockout drops?"

"Are you always this grumpy when you're tired?"

"Always. Well," she qualified her answer, "grumpy isn't exactly the right word."

"What would you call it?"

"I get honest. That fine line between saying what I think and being rude seems to get blurred."

"I see. Well, changing the subject back to sleeping..."

"I'm listening."

"The first thing you need to do is lean back and make yourself as comfortable as possible."

She settled into her seat and rested her head against the back of the seat. "All right."

"Close your eyes."

Eden obediently lowered her lids. "Now what?"

"Pick a nonsense word—something that means nothing to you at all—and repeat it in your mind over and over again."

Eden turned her head and gazed skeptically at Jack. "You're kidding."

"Trust me on this. It works every time."

She looked at him a moment longer before rearranging herself on her seat. "If you say so."

"Do you have your word yet?"

With her eyes closed once again, Eden gave it a moment's thought. "Yes."

"Now start saying it to yourself."

"I feel like an idiot," she muttered under her breath.

"Just do it."

"It's not going to work."

"Stop being so negative."

"You're right. I'm sorry. I'll give it an honest try."

"You'll have to stop talking."

A corner of her mouth lifted. "Yes, sir."

The plane suddenly jerked. Eden's eyes flew open. "What happened?"

"We landed."

The little plane raced over the dried grass and bumpy cracked earth until it came to a complete stop.

"Why did you land here? Is something wrong with the plane?"

"The plane is fine. This is where I live. You've been asleep for about three hours."

"No!" Eden was genuinely amazed.

"Yes!" He climbed out of the plane and walked around to her side to open the door. "Come on."

Eden put her hands on Jack's shoulders and slid gracefully out of her seat and into his arms. He lowered her slowly, holding her still for a heartbeat of time when they were at eye level, before setting her gently on the ground. Her hands quickly fell to her sides as she stepped away from him. "Thank you."

"You're welcome."

Eden cleared her throat. Her feet suddenly itched to walk away, but she remained still and tried to think of something to say. "It's not as hot as I expected it to be."

"That's because it's late in the day. The nights can be very pleasant."

"I see." She looked around. "What do we do now?"

"We get your luggage and drive to the house." He went past her and removed her suitcases from the plane, then walked to a Jeep that was parked nearby and hoisted them into the back. As he slid behind the steering wheel, Eden climbed in beside him. Jack reached to start the engine, but his hand suddenly stopped in midair. He looked around, took a deep breath and slowly exhaled. "I love coming home." His gaze rested on the woman beside him. "I hope you enjoy your time here, Eden."

"Thank you."

His gaze moved slowly over her face, feature by feature, before he wordlessly turned his attention back to his car and started it.

Eden had to force herself to look away from him as her thoughts raced along.

"You're being awfully quiet," he called to her over the loud noise of the engine as the Jeep bumped along the ground. "Having deep thoughts?"

"Remarkably shallow ones, actually."

"None of which you intend to share with me, right?"

"Oh, so right."

"Do you share your thoughts with Richard?"

Eden paused before she answered. "Some of them."

"Why not all of them?"

"Because I don't share all of my thoughts with anyone. Do you?"

"No. But I'm not supposed to be in love, either."

"Would that make a difference to you?"

Jack was quiet for a moment. "Yes," he finally said. "All the difference in the world."

"Are you saying that you'd be willing to share even the darkest corners of your mind?"

His teeth flashed white in his tanned face. "What do you know about dark corners?"

"Everyone has them. Even I." Her voice drifted as though she were talking to herself. "Places in our minds and hearts where we don't want to look too closely—much less let someone else look.''

Jack looked at Eden curiously. There was apparently more to her than she ordinarily let on.

As soon as they'd crossed over a slight incline and started down a narrow dirt road, Eden saw the house. It was large, square and white, with a wide, old-fashioned veranda that surrounded the house. There was no grass as a lawn, but there had been some attempt to create a garden, and a wrought-iron fence surrounded the garden and house to separate it from the rest of the property.

They passed fenced-in pastures; one, near a barn, contained over twenty horses who were running in a circle, kicking up dust. A mounted rider in the middle of the confusion spotted the Jeep and waved his hat at Jack as they passed.

''Who's that?''

''One of our stockmen.'' He drove another five hundred yards or so to the house and parked, then climbed out and got her luggage. ''This is it, Eden.''

She stepped out and looked around. ''Everything's so quiet. It looks deserted.''

''The others have probably already left.''

''Left?''

''We were all invited to a neighbour's home for a pre-wedding celebration.''

''And you had to pick me up. I'm sorry you had to miss it,'' she said sincerely.

He opened the gate for her and held it as she passed through, his eyes moving over her slender back. ''To be honest, I'm not much on parties. There's only so much small talk a man can make in one lifetime."

She turned and smiled at him. "Something tells me that you're underrating yourself."

"Not a chance, Eden." Jack moved past her and opened the front door. "I have a lot of faults but underrating myself isn't one of them."

Eden stepped past him into one of the loveliest homes she'd ever been in. It wasn't particularly elegant or showy, but slightly worn and comfortable with rich, highly polished wood that shone with the care it was given. The foyer was large with a faded Oriental rug covering the centre of the floor. A round table with a stunning sculpture of a rearing horse on it was positioned on the rug. A straight staircase with a banister—all the lovelier because of its plainness—led upstairs. An enormous grandfather clock sat in a place of honour on the landing. "This way," Jack told her as he headed up the stairs. "I had Mrs. Cleary make up a room for you at the far end of the house, away from the noise."

"Mrs. Cleary?"

"My housekeeper."

They walked in tandem down the long hallway until they came to the second-to-last door. Jack opened it and walked in, setting her luggage in a corner. He then crossed the room to the large windows and pushed back the shutters to let in the early evening air.

Eden loved the room as soon as she set eyes on it. There was an old-fashioned four-poster bed along one wall with elaborate carving on the headboard. The floor was wood, polished to a high gloss, with a centre square of thickly piled white carpeting. The walls were white. The colours in the room came from the blue bedspread and drapes and the dark wood of the furniture. "Bathroom's through there," Jack told her, pointing at a door. "Try to be a little conservative with how much water you use. We don't have any to waste."

She opened the door and looked in, delighting in the old-fashioned fixtures and the bathtub with feet. "All right."

"After you've had a chance to unpack and freshen up, we can either get something to eat here or go on to the party."

"I think I'd like to stay here, if you don't mind."

"Don't say that on my account. Regardless of what I said earlier, I'd be happy to take you."

"I know. The truth is I'd rather stay here and settle in. I've been travelling for days, and I'm not really in the mood for small talk, either."

A slow smile curved Jack's mouth as he looked at her. Eden responded to its charm against her will. "Good. I'll get cleaned up myself and start dinner."

Eden's gaze followed him to the door and stayed there long after he'd passed through it. She heard another door open and close not far away. Something about that man really bothered her. She wasn't looking forward to spending an entire evening alone with him, but Eden mentally shrugged her shoulders, she was just going to have to be pleasant and make the best of it. Crossing the room, Eden knelt on the cushioned window seat to look outside. There were numerous outbuildings and paddocks. And land. As far as the eye could see. It looked hostile to her. Hostile, yet beautiful in a frightening kind of way. How could anyone raise livestock out there? It seemed to her that it would be a never-ending battle between man and his environment.

And that somehow suited Jack Travers.

Eden raised both hands to her golden hair and removed the pins that held the elegant twist in place at the base of her neck. As it fell to her waist she rubbed her scalp where the pins had been and sighed.

Moving away from the window, Eden unpacked her things and, keeping in mind what Jack had said about the water supply, she undressed and showered very quickly, turning the water off while she soaped her long hair and on again to rinse it. When she'd finished blow-drying it her practised fingers twisted the strands into a French braid that started at her crown, then tucked the end up under the base of the braid at the nape of her neck, making her hair appear much shorter than it actually was. To hold it in place, she attached a bow of the same blue colour as the cotton skirt and short-sleeved blouse she pulled out of her luggage to wear. Her oval face was pale in the fading light and emphasised her large eyes. After putting a touch of rose-coloured lipstick on her mouth, Eden left her room and headed downstairs.

"There you are," Jack said as he entered the foyer from another room. "I thought perhaps you'd decided to rest."

"I'm more hungry than tired."

"How does an omelette sound?"

"Perfect."

"Come on, then, and give me a hand."

Eden followed him through the house to the kitchen. It was an open, friendly room, rich with the wood that was evident throughout the rest of the house. There was a fireplace along one wall, unlit now in the heat of the summer. All the appliances, which were every bit as modern as those in Eden's own kitchen, were designed along commercial proportions.

"Get eggs, milk and cheese out of the refrigerator," Jack told her as he took a skillet from its hook on the rack above the stove. She did as he asked and set the food on the counter, then on her own added butter and some ham. Working rather well as a team, considering it was their first time cooking together, Jack cracked the eggs into a bowl and beat them while Eden diced the ham and cheese. When everything was in the skillet, Jack poured two glasses of red wine and handed one to Eden, his eyes on hers as he raised his glass in a half-salute, saying nothing.

Eden returned the gesture and his look as they each took a sip. Her eyes searched his and she lowered her glass. "Why are you looking at me that way?" she asked quietly.

"What way?"

"As though you're trying to see inside me."

"Perhaps I am."

"I wish you wouldn't."

"What are you afraid of?"

"I'm not." As soon as she said the words, Eden knew she was lying.

So did Jack. Quite unexpectedly, he put his hands at her waist and lifted her on to the counter so that they were at eye level. "Why don't you want me to see inside you, Eden?"

"Why would you want to?"

"Don't answer a question with a question."

"I always do that when I don't want to answer a question with an answer."

Jack thought about her reply for a moment. "No one is more surprised than I am, but I actually understood that." He looked into her eyes. "So let me answer for you. You don't want me looking into your dark corners."

"That's right. No strangers allowed."

"What about friends?"

"You don't qualify."

"Will I ever?"

"Do you want to?"

"Want to and intend to." He put his hands at her waist again. Eden was wedged rather tightly between Jack and the counter, so that as he slowly lowered her to the ground, her body brushed against the length of his. As it had that night at the engagement party, the clean smell of him filled her senses. He reached around her, bringing their bodies into even closer contact. Eden's breath caught in her throat. Jack picked up his wineglass and took a drink, then set it back on the counter. "I think our dinner's ready," he said in his low voice as he moved away from her.

Eden, her heart racing, downed the rest of her wine in one gulp while Jack, with an ease that spoke of a man who'd done a lot of his own cooking, halved the omelette while it was still in the skillet and slid each section on to a separate plate. "It looks delicious," Eden told him conversationally, hoping her voice didn't show the stress she was feeling.

"I've set the table on the veranda," Jack told her as he lifted the plates. "I'll take these out and you bring the wine." He eyed Eden's empty glass as he walked past her. "Thirsty, are we?"

The way he'd said it was more teasing than condemning, and Eden found herself smiling as she picked up their two glasses in one hand, the bottle of wine in the other, and used her shoulder to push open the screen door leading to the veranda. Light from the kitchen window dully illuminated a table that could comfortably accommodate six people. Jack had positioned the plates so that he was at the head of the table, looking out over the land, and Eden was on his right. She set the glasses down and refilled hers. Jack held out her chair and Eden glanced over her shoulder at him in surprise. "Thank you."

"Were you expecting me to yank it out from under you?" he asked, his voice tinged with amusement as he took his own seat.

"I don't really know what to expect from you," Eden answered honestly, "except the unexpected."

"And you prefer predictability?"

"Oh, yes."

"Is that what you get from Richard?"

"Among other things." Eden flipped her napkin open and laid it across her lap as her eyes took in the moonlit surroundings. It was very peaceful—silent except for the distant sounds of animals and insects. Buildings and paddocks were outlined in the moonlight. "Do you eat out here often?" she asked as she took a bite of the melt-in-the-mouth omelette.

"Always, when the weather permits."

"What's a typical day like for you?"

Jack gazed at her over the rim of his wineglass. "Are you making polite conversation or do you really want to know?"

"I really want to know."

Jack set his glass on the table. "Instead of trying to explain things to you, how about if I take you out with me tomorrow?"

"Out where?"

"Around the station."

"Oh," she shook her head, "I don't think so."

"Why not?"

She couldn't very well tell him that she didn't want to be around him any more than she had to. "I'd just be in the way."

"True."

She looked at him in surprise and grinned suddenly. "Ouch."

"But it would only be for a day. If I can handle it, surely you can."

"A challenge?"

"If that's what you want to call it."

Eden thought about it for a moment. "All right. I'll do it."

Now it was Jack's turn to smile. "Good. Do you ride horses at all?"

"I did a lot of it when I was in boarding school."

"When was that?"

"From kindergarten on."

"Kindergarten? You're kidding. What kind of parents would put a five-year-old in boarding school?"

"Busy ones."

Jack could hear the withdrawal in her voice, so he dropped the subject. "Do you have anything to wear?"

"Not for riding."

"I'll dig up something for you by tomorrow."

"Thank you."

Jack inclined his head towards her empty plate. "Finished?"

"Yes. It was delicious."

"I'll clear away the dishes. You go on to bed. The day starts early around here."

"All right."

They rose together. Jack's gaze followed her to the door. "Eden?"

She stopped and turned.

He looked at Eden for a long moment as she stood there, framed by the light shining from behind her. "Goodnight."

She gazed back at him, her expression serious. "Goodnight, Jack."

When she'd gone Jack sat down again and stared at his land without really seeing it. Eden's image had haunted him since the night he'd met her, and now that she was here, in his most quiet moments, all he saw was her lovely face. She was different from any woman he'd ever met and as different from him as different could be. And yet her presence filled him with a strange kind of satisfaction, as though he'd been hungry without realising it until meeting her.

CHAPTER THREE

EDEN awoke to a knock on her door. Her eyes slowly focused on the bedside clock shining in the darkness. It was just a little after five. There was another knock. "Yes?" Her sleepy voice cracked, so she cleared her throat. "Who is it?"

"Jack."

She rose up on her elbows. "Jack?"

"May I come in?"

Protectively, Eden pulled her sheet higher. "Yes."

He opened the door and walked through the room to the windows, drawing back the drapes, opening the shutters and letting the orange glow of the sunrise in. "It's time to get up."

She looked at him as though he'd lost his mind. "Get up? You can't be serious. No one gets up at this hour." Eden lay back down and pulled the sheet over her head.

Jack walked over to the bed and familiarly gave her bottom a gentle swat through the sheet. "Come on. It's getting late and you aren't even dressed."

Eden lowered the sheet just enough so that she could fix him with a green-eyed glare. He was already dressed for work in jeans and a faded blue shirt. "I know I said I'd go with you this morning, but you didn't tell me that your version of morning was my version of middle of the night."

Jack leaned over the bed and looked into her eyes. "You'll love it once you're up."

"I find that hard to imagine."

"Trust me."

Eden sighed. "All right, all right. I'll get up."

"I put some clothes on the chair for you," he said as he straightened away from her and headed towards the door.

"Thank you." Eden uncovered the rest of her face.

"Mrs. Cleary's downstairs making breakfast. What would you like?"

"Breakfast?" She sounded every bit as appalled as she felt. "At this hour?"

The grooves in Jack's cheeks deepened. "We could always call it a midnight snack."

Eden smiled back at him, but it was a smile tinged with embarrassment. "Sorry. Morning isn't my best time. Toast would be nice."

"Then toast it is. I'll see you on the veranda in a few minutes."

When the door had closed behind him, Eden got out of bed and padded over to the windows to look out. The sun was almost but not completely up. Kind of like me, Eden thought. And already she could feel the heat.

It took her only a few minutes to wash and slip into the light cotton khaki-coloured pants and short-sleeved shirt with a pocket over each breast. There were even some brand-new sneakers that were only a half size too large. She brushed her hair out of its braid and put it into a ponytail high on her head.

When she got downstairs, she went straight outside to the veranda. Jack was already there drinking orange juice. He looked her over very thoroughly as she walked toward him. "The clothes are a good fit."

"Where did you find them?"

Jack rose and pulled the chair out for her. "They belong to Mrs. Cleary's granddaughter. She's only here once a year, so I don't think she'll mind your borrowing a few things. I sent to Alice Springs for the shoes late last night, and a friend of mine flew by this morning and dropped them off."

"Thank you for going to so much trouble."

"You're welcome. Want some juice?"

"Yes, please."

Eden watched his face as he poured a glass for her. "You're a very patient man."

A corner of his mouth lifted. "There are those who'd disagree."

"Well, with me you are. Or, at least, you have been so far."

His eyes met hers. There was something in their depths Eden couldn't quite read. "Drink your juice."

A tall, slender woman came onto the veranda, her short iron-grey hair in a profusion of curls, her tanned skin heavily lined. "You must be Miss Sloane," she said in a friendly, thickly accented voice. "I'm Mrs. Cleary."

Eden extended her hand. "Hello, Mrs. Cleary. Thank you for the clothes."

The housekeeper squeezed her hand. "No worries. And there are more where those came from if they're needed." She put a plate of warm toast in front of Eden. "Now, what's this about you just having toast for breakfast? That's not much to eat for a full working morning on the station. Sure I can't fix you something else?"

"Thanks, but I don't have much of an appetite this early in the day."

"Well, if you change your mind, give me a call." She turned to Jack. "I forgot to tell you that Jillie stopped by yesterday while you were off in Sydney."

"Did she say what she wanted?"

"We both know the answer to that one, don't we now?"

"Mrs. Cleary..."

She raised her hand. "Never you mind. I've given you my opinion on that one before. I expect she'll be back today." With another look, Mrs. Cleary went into the house.

"What was that all about?" Eden asked curiously as she bit into her toast.

"Nothing important."

"Who's Jillie?"

"Jillie Morgan. She's a neighbour."

"And Mrs. Cleary doesn't like her," Eden guessed.

"She likes her. It's impossible not to like Jillie."

"Then what is it?"

"Let's just say she doesn't think Jillie is the right woman for me."

"What do you think?"

"I think," he said after a thoughtful moment's pause, "that a man could do worse."

"Are you going to marry her?" Eden realised even as she asked the question that she was torn about what she wanted his answer to be.

Jack raised an expressive brow. "For someone who doesn't like to answer personal questions herself, you sure don't seem to mind asking them."

"I have a shocking set of double standards, I know," she agreed, undaunted. "Are you?"

Jack finished his juice, set the glass on the table and looked Eden in the eye. "No. I'm not in love with her and I can't see that changing now." He inclined his head toward her glass. "Finish your juice and bring your toast along. We have to get going."

Eden quickly drank what was left and took the last corner of toast.

Jack picked up a hat from the seat of the chair next to him and plopped it on Eden's head. With hands that gently brushed her skin, he tightened the chin strap for her. "Wear that whenever you're outside."

"All right."

"And put some of this on." He handed her a tube of sunscreen. "With that fair skin of yours, you should probably start bathing in the stuff."

"What's the temperature supposed to be today?"

"About 115 degrees."

Eden's eyes widened. "That's obscene."

"Kind of like winter in New York to someone from here. You'll get used to it."

"Not in this life."

Jack stood and pulled out her chair for her. "Ready?"

She looked up at him. "One hundred fifteen?"

"One hundred fifteen."

She sighed. "As ready as I'll ever be."

Together they walked down the veranda steps and through the small garden to the smooth dirt road that led to a paddock and stables. A ranch hand was in the paddock working some horses. He stopped when he saw them and rode over to the fence. "G'day, Jack. Miss." He politely doffed his sweat-stained hat and jammed it back on his head.

Jack walked over to the fence and rested his foot on the bottom rung. "Les, I'd like you to meet Eden Sloane. She's going to be a guest here for a few days."

"In for the wedding, are you?" he asked.

"That's right."

He eyed her appreciatively up and down, but it was strangely inoffensive. "Carn! Any more like you back home?"

Eden just smiled at him in a silent acknowledgment of the compliment.

"Les, mind your manners."

"No worries, boss." His tone was good-natured as he turned his attention from Eden to Jack. "I've been thinking that we might take some of the beasts a bit north today and see if we have a little better luck with the water from that bore."

"I'll go out there later to see how things look."

"All right, but we can't put it off too much longer. Things are drying up everywhere." Les inclined his head towards Eden and turned his horse back into the paddock.

Jack didn't say anything as they walked into the stables. He led a horse out for her, a chestnut mare, and then his own horse, a jet-black thoroughbred. "Do you remember how to saddle one from your days at boarding school?"

"I think I can manage." She sounded more confident than she felt.

"Use the gear to the right of the stall door."

As soon as Eden saw the equipment, everything came back to her. She finished saddling a few minutes after Jack. He walked around to her mare and gave her a leg up, then mounted his own horse and rode through the large double doors of the stable. Eden drew up alongside him. They rode quietly for about fifteen minutes down the same track they'd driven along the day before. He veered off when they were about half a mile from the house and rode over dried-out pasture. Gum trees rose out of the stark landscape, some of them long dead, others barely alive. They rode for nearly two hours along a fence, with Jack making note of where repairs needed to be made, before stopping next to a dusty gash in the earth that used to be a stream.

Jack climbed off his horse and caught Eden around the waist to help her down. "Thirsty?" he asked.

Eden made a determined effort to ignore the way her body reacted to his touch. "My throat's like a desert." She pulled her shirt-tail up and wiped the perspiration from her forehead. She'd never experienced the kind of suffocating heat that surrounded her now. It hurt to breathe.

Jack took a pouch from his saddle and handed it to her. "Just drink straight from it," he told her when he saw that she was looking for something to pour it in. He raised another one to his own lips, and Eden watched the smooth muscles of his throat move rhythmically as he drank deeply. He suddenly raised the pouch from his mouth to his face and splashed the still cool water over his hot skin and shook his head.

Eden took a more delicate drink from her pouch, then poured some into the palm of one hand and rubbed it over her flushed and dusty face. Only a few hours earlier, she wouldn't have believed how wonderful a little water could feel.

Jack then cupped one hand, poured a steady stream of water into it and held it under his horse's mouth. Eden did the same thing.

"How's your backside holding up to the riding?" he asked Eden suddenly.

Frankly, between having her legs stretched around the horse for hours and her rear end bounced in the saddle until it was beyond pain, Eden thought she was going to die. But she wasn't about to tell him that. "Just fine," she said with a too-bright smile.

He glanced sceptically at her.

"Really." She tried to sound convincing, but it didn't come off even to her own ears.

"If you say so." Jack gathered the reins of the two horses and tethered them to a tree, then took Eden by the hand and led her to the shade of a small tree. "Let's rest here for a few minutes."

"You don't have to do that on my account."

"Then let's do it on mine. I want to get out of the sun." He sat down, took off his hat and wiped the sweat from his forehead with his shirtsleeve. "It's too bloody hot."

Eden grimaced as she eased herself onto the ground next to him, unaware of the amused glance Jack sent her way. "I should think you'd be used to the heat," she told him when she'd finally, blessedly, reached the ground.

"Just because you get used to it doesn't mean you get to liking it." He studied her lovely profile. "You asked me some personal questions earlier. Now it's my turn."

Instantly, Eden became wary.

"Are you really going to marry that Richard character?"

"That Richard character?" she repeated. "You make him sound less than human."

"I just can't picture you with him."

She drew a circle in the dust with her forefinger. "Most people think we make a perfect couple."

"Perfect-looking. The two of you could model for the top of a wedding cake."

"Why don't I think that's a compliment?"

"Because it's not. There's no real emotion between the two of you."

"You saw us together for all of five minutes."

"All right, tell me this. Why are you marrying him?"

Eden paused thoughtfully. "He's a very nice man," she finally said.

"And?" Jack pressed when she'd been silent for several seconds. "What else?"

"What do you mean, what else?"

"That's it?" he asked in amazement. "That's all you can come up with? He's a very nice man? Hardly what I'd call either a recommendation for marriage or a resounding declaration of love."

Eden grew silent.

"Are you in love with him, Eden?"

She chose her words carefully. "I'm very fond of Richard. Very, very fond."

"But do you love him, Eden?"

She turned her head and looked into Jack's eyes for a long moment, then looked away. "I don't know."

"Then why would you even think of marriage?"

"Perhaps," she said after a long silence, "I care as much about Richard as I'm capable of caring about anyone. And perhaps I'm not looking for a grand passion. Richard is predictable and nice, and he makes me feel safe."

"You mean to say that with him you're in no danger of losing that self-control you wrap yourself in like a blanket."

Eden rose to her feet and brushed the dust from her pants. "Where to now?" she asked, effectively closing the subject.

Jack rose also and stood looking down at her. "Back to the station," he answered, taking her less-than-subtle hint. He walked down into the dry river-bed and dug at the cracked earth with the toe of his boot. "There's always been water here before. One of the men told me yesterday that the river was dry, but I had to see it for myself." He gazed straight into the sun and sighed. "It has to rain soon, Eden. It has to."

"Are you going to move the cattle if it doesn't?"

"I'll have no choice." He climbed up the bank and untethered the horses. "I'm flying to the north range when we get back. Want to come with me?"

Eden hesitated before answering. Sometimes she felt as though having a conversation with him was like walking through a minefield. He probed too much. "On the condition that we don't talk about anything personal."

"Agreed."

"All right, then. I'd like to."

Jack, smiling to himself, gave her a boost into her saddle and mounted his own horse. The self-assured Eden Sloane was nervous around him. That was good. It beat the hell out of indifference. "Now, how is your backside holding up?"

Eden tried not to smile, but she couldn't quite suppress it as her eyes met his. "All right, I'll admit it. The truth is that I'm not going to walk normally for a week."

"Maybe even two," he suggested. The words were just something to keep his mouth busy while he looked at her. Every once in a while he could see the cracks in her shield. It was just for a moment, but they were there. For all that she was determined to take care of herself and not lean on anyone else, there was something about her—something deep inside her—that made Jack want to pull her into his arms and protect her.

A small frown creased Eden's forehead. "Jack? You're looking at me strangely. Did I say something wrong?"

He forced a smile. "No. I was just thinking."

"Not very happy thoughts, I take it."

"Disquieting."

"Anything I can help with?"

He turned his horse in the direction of the station. "No. Let's get home."

The ride back was, if possible, even hotter than it had been earlier. Eden couldn't imagine how people could live under these conditions. How could anything even exist in this heat?

They paused only once to water the horses—and themselves. As they approached the stables, Eden suddenly stopped and stared into a corral that was empty except for one white stallion. He was one of the most exquisite creatures Eden had ever seen with his arched neck and aristocratic bearing.

Jack reined in next to her. "Handsome, isn't he?"

Eden was silent for a moment before turning to Jack. "He's beautiful."

"Beth had the same reaction when she saw him. In fact, she offered to buy him."

"Did you sell him to her?"

"No."

"Then sell him to me."

He looked at her in surprise. "To you? Where would you keep a horse?"

"Not for me. As my wedding present to Beth. She loves horses, and she and David are going to be living in Australia."

"That would be kind of an expensive gift."

Eden looked back at the horse. "But worth every penny. What's his name?"

"Savato. It's Greek for 'Saturday,' the day he was born."

"Why Greek?"

"His sire was from Athens."

Eden's eyes roamed over the beautiful creature then turned to Jack. "Will you sell him to me?"

He hesitated for just a moment. "I'm afraid not."

"I'll pay whatever you want."

"It's not the money, Eden. I just don't want to part with the horse."

There was nothing Eden liked better than a challenge. "I'm used to getting what I want."

"Not this time."

"All right for now," she said, wheeling her mare around and riding off, "but I won't give up without a fight."

Neither will I, Jack thought as he turned his horse and rode beside her into the stables.

Eden winced as she slid to the ground. "What's next?" she asked as she unsaddled her horse.

"Lunch and flying to the north pasture."

"Oh, that's right. You mentioned that earlier."

Jack hung his saddle on a hook and turned to Eden. "You don't have to go if you don't want to. It's been a long morning."

"That's all right." She lifted her saddle and hung it next to his, then wiped her sweating palms on her pants. "Besides, after that ride, sitting on a plane will seem like heaven."

As they walked from the dimly lit barn into the sunlight, they saw a Jeep kicking up dust as it sped toward them and stopped just ahead of them in a cloud. A woman sat behind the steering wheel, her short brown hair in a modern jagged cut around her cute, tanned face. "G'day, Jack."

"Jillie." Jack inclined his head.

Her friendly brown eyes went to Eden. "You must be the bride-to-be."

"Actually, this is Eden Sloane. She's a good friend of Beth's."

Eden smiled and held out her hand. "How do you do, Jillie."

Jillie's own smile faded and was replaced by a look of interest as she shook Eden's hand. Her eyes swung back to Jack. "I stopped by yesterday."

"So Mrs. Cleary told me. I was off in Sydney. What did you want?"

"Since when does a neighbour need a reason to drop in on a neighbour?"

"You know you don't, Jillie."

Eden quietly watched the two of them. It was obvious that Jillie had strong feelings for Jack. Physically speaking, they were a beautifully matched couple, both tanned and healthy-looking with athletic builds.

"Actually," Jillie amended pleasantly, "there was something, but it's station business. I see no reason to bore Eden with it. Perhaps we could talk later."

Eden picked up the hint. "I have a better idea. I'll go on up to the house to get something to drink, and you two have your talk now." She smiled at Jack. "Come get me when you're ready to leave." Extending her hand again, she turned to Jillie. "It was nice meeting you."

"Likewise."

Eden was unaware of the two gazes following her as she walked toward the house and through the gate. She noticed only the beckoning shade of the veranda—where it was probably only a hundred and five degrees. Instead of going in the front door, she followed the porch around to the kitchen entrance. The housekeeper looked up from dicing carrots and smiled at the sight of her. "You look hot."

"I *feel* hot," she admitted, sighing as she sank onto a counter stool with a wince of pain.

Mrs. Cleary wiped her hands off on her apron as she walked to the refrigerator, filled a glass with ice and popped the cap off a cold bottle of mineral water. "Here," she said as she set them in front of Eden. "This should cool you down a little."

"Thank you." Eden poured the sparkling clear liquid over the cubes, and held the glass first to one flushed cheek and then the other before drinking deeply. "I never knew water could taste so wonderful."

"If you want some more, just yell."

Eden sat for a few moments, listening to the quiet. "Where is everyone?"

"Sleeping. They didn't even get home from the party until just before you got up this morning."

"Must have been a good party."

"They all are out here. Is Jack coming back soon?"

"He's outside talking with a neighbour."

"Jillie?"

"Umhm."

"Well, I hope she doesn't keep him too long. I have his lunch ready." She glanced at Eden. "You must be starving, considering the breakfast you ate."

"I am."

"Get one of those covered plates from the sideboard. I hope you like cold roast-beef sandwiches."

"At this point," Eden told the housekeeper over her shoulder as she got the plate, "I like anything that's cold. Where can I wash?"

"Right there at the sink."

Eden put the plate next to her glass, then went to the sink and splashed cold water on her face before generously soaping her hands and arms and rinsing them off under the tap.

"Here you go."

She turned to find Jack standing there, holding a towel out to her.

"Thank you. I thought you were still outside."

"We finished our business."

"Is Jillie staying for lunch?" Mrs Cleary asked.

"No. She had to go home. Eden and I will be taking our food with us on the plane." Jack went to the sink Eden had just vacated and washed himself off while the housekeeper busily packed the food and some beverages into a small basket.

Eden finished the last of her mineral water just as Jack turned to her, drying himself off with another towel. "Ready?"

"Ready."

He tossed the towel onto the counter. Walking over to Eden, he raised her hat from where it hung down her back and plopped it onto her head. "Now you're ready. See you later, Mrs. Cleary," he called to the housekeeper as he picked up the basket and headed out the door, with Eden close on his heels.

Almost before Eden was in her seat, Jack gunned the Jeep down the dirt track to where the little plane patiently waited, baking in the sun.

"You get the basket," Jack told her as he brought the Jeep to a stop next to the plane, "while I air her out a bit." He hopped out and opened both doors of the plane, then climbed into the pilot's seat and started the engine. "Come on," he called, signalling to her from inside.

Eden stowed the small basket in the area behind their seats then climbed in, fastened her seat belt and pulled her door closed. The air conditioning was already cooling things off. Within moments, Jack had turned the plane around and sped down the dirt runway. Eden felt an odd kind of excitement as the plane bounced along the ground, picking up speed, then suddenly lifted into the air and soared to the right, arcing over the house. "How far away are we going?" she asked above the noise of the engines.

"About half an hour from here."

"That covers a lot of ground. How large is your station?"

"Five hundred thousand acres, give or take a thousand."

"That's huge!"

"Not for out here. And particularly not when you consider that at least half the land is uninhabitable."

"Did it used to belong to your parents?"

"No, though some of the money I inherited from them went into the purchase of the place eight years ago."

"Do your brothers own it with you?"

"No. David wasn't interested, and Terry'd spent all his money by the time this place came on the market. Get out the sandwiches and hand me one, will you?"

Eden obligingly reached behind their seats for the basket and propped it open on her lap. "Here," she said as she unwrapped one and handed him half of it. "What would you like to drink?"

"Water's fine."

She popped the cap off two bottles of mineral water and set them in the corner of the basket, then went to work on the other half of the sandwich. "This is delicious," she said after swallowing her first bite.

Jack looked over at her and smiled. "Food always tastes better when you've earned an appetite."

"Apparently. I normally don't even like roast beef." She handed him his water and looked out of the plane. "I'm even starting to enjoy the scenery."

"You sound surprised."

"I am, frankly. This just isn't me."

"What is you, Eden?"

"Tall buildings, bright lights . . ."

"Are you sure that's the life you prefer?"

"It's the only one I've ever known."

"Until now."

She looked at him and smiled, relaxing with him despite herself. "Until now," she agreed.

"Do you have any brothers or sisters?"

"No."

"What about your parents? Are they still living?" He sensed rather than saw her withdraw as soon as he'd asked the question.

"They're alive." Eden leaned more towards the window. "What's that cloud of dust in the distance?"

He looked at her profile for a moment, wanting to find out why she'd had that reaction, but knowing better than to press her. "That's the herd."

The dust seemed to stretch across the horizon as far as the eye could see. "What happens now?"

Jack finished his water and put the bottle back into the basket. "I land this thing."

Eden closed up the basket and put it behind their seats, then watched as Jack circled around the herd to a smooth stretch of land below and landed without incident. "You wait near the plane," he told her as he climbed out. "I won't be long."

Eden stepped out onto the wing and watched. Jack had walked less than a hundred yards when three dust-covered men rode up on dust-covered horses and dismounted to speak with him. She stayed there for a few minutes, but the heat reflecting up from the white wing grew to be too much, and she jumped to the ground.

As she stood there, Eden thought she heard a noise and grew very still to listen. For several moments there was nothing, then the faintest of moans. Or was it a moan? She'd never heard anything quite like it. Leaving the shelter of the plane, she headed towards a thicket about ten yards away, stopping every few steps to listen. The sound grew a little louder. Stepping very carefully, she walked into the thicket, still moving towards the noise—albeit a little nervously—when she found the source. A small calf that looked almost newborn was tangled in some scrub. It had fallen onto its side and its gangly legs weakly kicked the air. "Oh, you poor baby," Eden said in a rich, calming tone as she approached. "I'll get you out of there."

It looked at her with wide, terrified eyes.

"Shh," she said as she knelt beside the calf and gently stroked her. "What have you gotten yourself into?"

"Eden! Where are you?"

"Over here, Jack."

"Keep talking so I can follow your voice."

"I'm in the thicket. There's a calf here. I think she might be injured, but I won't be able to tell until I get her untangled from the vines."

Jack knelt down next to her. "Don't ever do that again."

"Do what?" she asked in surprise.

"Walk into an overgrown area like this."

"But I heard the calf..."

"I don't care what you heard. Snakes thrive in places like this."

She looked at him in horror, then her eyes went to the ground. "Snakes?"

"Deadly ones." He turned his attention to the calf and sadly stroked its head. "I'm afraid she's had it."

Eden forgot about the snakes. "What do you mean?"

"Her leg's injured, she's dehydrated and her mother's nowhere around."

"So we'll fix her leg, give her something to drink and find her mother." It all seemed a simple enough thing to her.

"It doesn't work that way. Picking her mother out of a herd that size would be like trying to find a needle in a haystack. The kindest thing we can do for the baby is destroy it.''

''No!''

''There's nothing else we can do.''

''There most certainly is. We can untangle her and take her home with us.''

''In the plane?''

''She's little. There's plenty of room.''

''Eden . . .''

She looked at him with pleading eyes that were impossible to resist. Her guard was well and truly down. ''Please, Jack. Just give her a chance.''

Without saying anything else, Jack set about untangling the weak calf. Once it was free, he lifted it in his arms and carried it to the plane. Still not believing he was actually doing this, he waited until Eden had climbed in before gently loading the calf. It lay on the floor of the plane, directly at Eden's feet, barely able to raise its head. Eden's eyes met Jack's. ''Thank you,'' she said softly.

The tenderness in his gaze warmed her. ''You're welcome. Just don't be too hurt if it dies.''

''She won't die. I won't let her.''

''Things don't always go the way we want them to. Particularly out here.''

''And how do you want things to go?'' she asked before she realised that she wasn't talking about the calf.

Jack's gaze roamed over her lovely, dusty face. "I'm all for a happy ending—even if it's not quite the happy ending I was expecting." He looked at her for a moment longer, then closed the door and walked around to his side.

CHAPTER FOUR

As THEY drove the Jeep past the house, Jack spotted Terry reading on the veranda and stopped. "Terry, call Doc Murphy and tell him we have a very sick calf. We'll be in the barn."

Terry put down his newspaper and got to his feet. "Right. Anything else?"

"Find one of Mrs. Cleary's rubber gloves—the ones she uses for scrubbing—make sure it's clean and bring it to the barn with some milk."

"I'll be right there, faster than you can say—"

Eden didn't hear what it would be faster than, because Jack took off for the barn before Terry finished his sentence. The barn, a huge natural wood structure not too far from the stables, sat as though waiting for them, its sky-high double doors gaping open. Jack drove straight into the building and stopped halfway through. Scooping the calf from Eden's lap into his arms, he laid it gently on a soft mound of fresh hay.

"Is there anything I can do?" Eden asked as she hovered like an anxious mother over Jack's shoulder.

"Not right now. But as soon as Terry gets here, we can try feeding her."

Right on cue, Terry came running in, rubber glove and milk in hand. "I got hold of Doc Murphy. He said he could be here in an hour or so."

"Where is he?"

"At the Tracy place." He kneeled next to his brother. "What happened to this little fellow?"

"I'm not sure," Jack said as he took the glove. "It either got separated from the herd, or its mother just left it to die when she saw how weak it was."

"Maybe that's what you should have done as well. It's going to cost you more to have the doc here than this calf's ever going to be worth—in the unlikely event it even survives—if this drought keeps up."

Jack turned his head and his eyes met Eden's. She had such a look of vulnerability about her. "It'll survive."

A soft smile curved Eden's mouth, and Jack felt his heart catch at the power it had over him.

Terry looked at her, also. "So, this is your doing. Leave it to a woman to take the least logical path."

"You mean," she said quietly, altering his words as she kneeled between the two men, "leave it to a woman to do the right thing. What are you going to do with that glove, Jack?"

"I want to try to get the calf to take some nourishment."

"I figured that's what it was for," Terry told him, "so I punctured the tip of one of the fingers with a needle."

Jack filled the glove with milk and held the finger on which a drip formed to the calf's mouth, moistening it. The calf didn't respond at all. It just lay there, looking at them with its huge, terrified eyes.

"Come on, sweetheart," Eden coaxed softly as she stroked its forehead. "Just taste it."

Jack handed the glove to her. "Keep trying. There's something I need to take care of. Terry," he said as he got to his feet, "listen for Doc Murphy's plane. As soon as you hear it, pick him up in the Jeep."

"No probs." As soon as Jack had gone, Terry began stroking the calf. "She is a pretty little thing, isn't she?" he said softly, his heart obviously touched despite his apparent gruffness.

Eden looked up from what she was doing long enough to smile. "I thought you were supposed to be a tough guy?"

"If you tell anyone I've got a heart, I'll deny it." He grew alert suddenly and raised his head to listen. "Hear that?"

Eden listened also. "It sounds like a plane."

"Must be the doc. I'll be back in half a mo," he called to her as he jumped into the Jeep and skilfully gunned it backwards out of the barn.

With a sigh, Eden rearranged herself on the straw next to the calf, gently placing its head on her lap. It struggled just a moment, then grew still as if it suddenly recognised that it didn't need to fight her. Eden gently rubbed the milky glove finger against its mouth. "Just taste it, sweetheart. Forget about your mother. You don't need her. I know it hurts to be deserted, but you have me now."

Jack, who had moments earlier entered the barn, stopped and listened.

"I'm going to help you get better, but you have to help yourself, too."

Terry pulled up in the Jeep, parking it just outside the barn. Doc Murphy, a big, burly man whose rust-red hair had started to go gray, climbed out and hastened to the calf. Kneeling next to Eden, he ran his thick but surprisingly sensitive fingers over every inch of the calf, looked in its mouth and eyes, ears and nose, then concentrated his attention on its injured foreleg.

Jack helped Eden to her feet and stood there with his arm around her while they watched the doctor.

"This leg's going to be fine," he finally pronounced as he put some salve on the wound and carefully wrapped it. "Nothing's broken or sprained. Of course, if she doesn't take in some nourishment soon, the leg won't matter one way or the other." He wiped his hands on a clean cloth from his bag and stood up.

"Any suggestions?" Jack asked.

The doctor inclined his head towards the glove Eden was holding. "What you're doing is fine. Keep trying every hour or so to get her to drink. The rest is up to the calf. I'll stop back tomorrow to see how she's doing." He picked up his bag and turned to Terry. "Get me back to my plane. I have three more stops to make."

Eden stood there looking at the calf, then turned her gaze to Jack. "Is that it? I thought he'd be able to do more. He didn't even try to get her to eat."

"He's a doctor, not a miracle worker." Jack pushed the stray hair away from Eden's hot face and cupped her cheek in his hand. "Go on to the house and get cleaned up for dinner."

"I can't leave . . ."

"I'll stay here until I can get one of my men to take my place. You don't need to worry about a thing. Someone will be with her for the entire night."

Eden suddenly reached up and kissed his cheek, then pulled back, her eyes on his. "Thank you." Leaning down, she gently touched the calf. "I'll be back," she said softly.

Jack watched her leave, unaware that he himself was being watched. Glove in hand, he hunkered beside the calf. Terry walked in and stood looking down at his brother, his hands on his hips. "Don't do it, Jack."

"Don't do what?" he asked absently.

"Fall in love with her."

"You're giving me advice about women?" he said drily. "That's an interesting switch."

"I'm giving you advice about *this* woman." Terry knelt beside his brother. "Eden's wonderful, but you can take it from me, she's all wrong for you."

"That's for me to decide."

"If you have to fall in love, for God's sake pick a woman born to this kind of life."

Jack looked his brother in the eye. "Back off, Terry. It's none of your business."

Terry raised his hand. "All right. I won't bring it up again, but I hope you'll think about it."

Eden stepped out of the shower and toweled her hair, then blew it dry as she brushed it in long, slow strokes.

As she left the bathroom, still wrapped in a towel, Beth knocked on her door and walked in. "There you are!" She hugged Eden and sat on the bed. "I'm sorry I wasn't here when you arrived yesterday, but David really wanted to go to that party."

"That's all right. Jack and I had a nice dinner, and I got to bed early for a change." She walked to her closet and pulled out a white linen skirt and blouse. "How's this for dinner?"

"Perfect."

With the comfortableness of friends who had spent years together in boarding schools, Eden slipped out of her towel and into her clothes while Beth relaxed back on the pillows, her hands behind her head, and talked. "I understand you met Jillie today."

"Um-hm. This morning." Eden tucked in her blouse and reached into her drawer for a wide belt.

"What did you think of her?"

"She seemed nice."

"She's coming to dinner tonight."

Eden looked at her friend out of the corner of her eye. "Why do I get the feeling you're trying to provoke some kind of response other than she seemed nice, out of me?"

"Because I am."

"Why?"

Beth innocently inspected her nails. "No reason."

Eden picked up a box of hairpins and a brush from her dresser and sat on the bed with Beth. "Do something with my hair, will you? I'm tired of playing with it."

Beth sat up and started brushing through the thick strands. "I love your hair. Why don't you just leave it down? That's what I'd do if it were mine."

"I look like a teenager."

"What's wrong with that?"

"I'm too old to look like a teenager."

Beth was silent for a few minutes as she twisted Eden's hair this way and that and inserted pins to hold it. "Why didn't Richard come with you?"

"He was held up by business."

"Again."

Eden turned to her friend. "I'm really sorry, Beth, and so's Richard. He would have come if he could have. You know how fond of you he is."

Beth didn't say anything.

"Why are you being so quiet?"

Beth seemed to wage a battle within herself and lost. "I know you don't like to listen to criticism of Richard, but just this once hear me out. I was talking to my analyst about you the other day, and he said—"

"You talked to your analyst about me?"

Beth tugged Eden's hair. "Stop moving your head. That's right—about you. And he's concerned."

"Oh, Beth."

"I'm not kidding. He's really worried about you. He thinks that marrying Richard is your way of not facing reality."

Eden's eyes met Beth's in the mirror across the room. "You know as well as anyone that I've been facing reality since I was born."

"That's just it. Think about it, Eden. How many Christmases did you spend alone at school because your parents couldn't tear themselves away from their pleasure of the moment long enough to be with you? If I hadn't come back to school early that one year and found you there, I never would have known that you had nowhere to go. I was your best friend, and you never said a word."

"I was embarrassed. I didn't want anyone to feel sorry for me." She smiled faintly at the memory. "I'm glad you found out, though. The Christmases I spent with you and your family after that meant—and still mean—the world to me."

Beth put the last pin into Eden's elegant twist and rested her chin on Eden's shoulder as their eyes met once again in the mirror. "Honey, I'm the only one you've ever let see the real Eden Sloane. You have so much to give that you're almost bursting with it, but you won't let yourself because it means a loss of control, and with a loss of control comes real feelings and the chance of rejection and pain. Richard is a nice man and he'll probably never hurt you—but the reason he'll never hurt you is because you don't really love him. Nothing about him even begins to dent that armor of control you surround yourself with."

"Beth, you're as close to me as a sister ever could be. Thank you for caring. But I think I'm the best judge of how I feel. I gave my decision to marry Richard a lot of thought, and I believe we'll have a nice life together."

Beth kissed Eden on the cheek. "All right. Just think about what I've said. Please." Beth smiled into the mirror and Eden smiled back at her.

"Now," Eden said as she rose from the bed, "enough about me. How are you doing with the pre-wedding jitters?"

"I'm a wreck!"

"Have you been able to get in touch with your parents yet?"

"No. Have you ever tried to contact someone in China when you weren't sure exactly where they were? It's impossible."

"You could postpone the wedding," Eden suggested.

"Oh no." Beth shook her head. "I know they're going to be disappointed, but I love David and I want to be his wife now. Besides, this way we can keep the ceremony small and private. You know how Mom and Dad are." Her voice held deep affection. "Everything has to be larger than life." She watched as Eden put on earrings. "You need to add a little colour to your cheeks."

Eden grinned at her. "I'm really going to miss your lovely mothering."

"You won't have to. I'll just do it long distance." She looped her arm through Eden's. "Let's go face the madding crowd."

When they got downstairs the others had left the cool sanctuary of the house to sit on the veranda. Jack wasn't there yet. Terry was on the porch swing next to Jillie, laughing and rocking gently back and forth.

Beth walked over to David and kissed him soundly on the mouth. "Did you miss me, handsome?"

"Desperately."

Watching the two of them gave Eden a warm feeling. Smiling, she found a comfortable chair and sank onto it. It was only when she was halfway down that she realised she was going too fast and gasped as her sore muscles protested.

"Fun day out on the range, eh, Eden?" Terry asked from across the veranda, a mischievous grin lighting his face.

She smiled back at him. "I guess I can't fool you."

"Not with the obvious. You look rooted."

"Rooted?"

"You know. Tired."

"Oh! For a minute I thought you were being obscene."

His smile grew larger. "I can see I'm going to have to watch you."

"Don't pay any attention to him," Jillie told her. "He's under the impression—mistaken impression, might I add—that he's amusing. So, what did you think of your first day on an Australian cattle station?"

"It was ... interesting."

"A lot different from what you're used to, I imagine."

"Different, yes, but in a nice way. The heat's horrible, though."

"Yeah, well, at least it's not that way all year long. Just half of it."

Jack came out of the house dressed in loose white pants with pleats in the front and a white and blue striped shirt with the sleeves rolled halfway up his forearms. His long hair was still damp from the shower and curled slightly in the back. His eyes went straight to Eden, and he walked over to her and sat on the arm of her chair. "The calf still hasn't eaten anything," he told her in a quiet voice, "but she's in very capable hands for the night. You don't have to worry about her."

"Thank you."

"How are you feeling?"

"Rooted."

A corner of his mouth lifted. "I see you've been talking to Terry."

"I've been *listening* to Terry."

"Are you sore?"

"Let's just say that I'm not sure I can get out of this chair without help."

Mrs. Cleary came out with a tray of drinks holding everything from lemonade to beer and wine.

"What do you think you'd like, Eden?" Jack asked as he walked to the tray.

"Lemonade, please."

He poured two glasses, handed her one and kept one for himself. "I saw the stock today," he told Terry as he leaned the backs of his legs against the railing.

"And?"

"They're thirsty. Grazing is getting sparse. We're going to have to move them in the next few days."

Terry nodded. "I thought as much. Too damn bad, really. It's going to be a hard trip for them."

"There's not much else we can do."

"I can loan out some of our men," Jillie offered. "I'm sure my father won't mind."

"Thanks. We just might need them."

"You can count on me," said David.

Jack shook his head and smiled. "Not this time. You're going to be on your honeymoon."

"We can postpone it." Beth elbowed him sharply, but David was unrepentant. "We can, Jack."

"That's not necessary, David, but I appreciate the offer. Terry and I can handle things here, especially if Jillie can cut loose a few men."

Eden listened with interest as she sipped her lemonade. There was such a sense of camaraderie among the three brothers. This was what family was all about. Her gaze went to Jack and rested there. He was very much a product of his environment; long, lean, tanned and relaxed. Terry said something funny and Jack laughed. It was a deep rich sound that flowed inside Eden and warmed her. That warmth shone in her eyes. Beth saw it; Terry saw it; and when Jack's gaze turned to Eden, he saw it, too.

Mrs. Cleary came onto the veranda at that moment. "Dinner's ready."

"It's about time," Terry said, slapping his thigh. "I'm hungry enough to eat a horse and chase the jockey."

Without taking his eyes from Eden, Jack walked over to her and held out his hand. "Thought you might need a little help."

"Thank you," she said gratefully as she put her hand into his and let him pull her to her feet. "I didn't know it was possible to be this sore and live."

"In a few days you won't even notice it."

"Ah, something to look forward to."

With his hand placed protectively in the small of her back, he guided Eden around the veranda to the same table where they'd breakfasted so many hours earlier and seated her to his right at the head of the table. Beth sat with David and Jillie with Terry. The conversation flowed, and once again, Eden spent more time listening than talking and thoroughly enjoyed herself.

By the time the meal was over, though, she was half-asleep. Jack touched her arm and leaned towards her. "Do you want to go to your room? You got kind of an early start this morning."

She looked at him apologetically. "I'm sorry. I didn't realise I was being so obvious," she said softly.

"Only to me."

There was something intimate in the way he said that. "What about the calf?"

"I'll check on her before I go to bed, and someone will stay with her for the night."

"Thank you."

"You're welcome. Sleep well."

She looked around the table as she rose. "Excuse me, everyone, but I'm a little tired."

Terry and David both rose.

Beth reached up and kissed Eden on the cheek. "I'll see you early in the morning, Eden. We have some major pre-wedding planning to do."

"All right." She smiled at Jillie. "Good night." Eden walked in through the kitchen and said goodnight to Mrs. Cleary, then went upstairs to her room. After slipping out of her clothes she hung them in the closet and pulled out her long, old-fashioned white cotton nightgown. She loved the loose fit. After she'd taken all the pins out of her hair and brushed it, she flipped off the light and lay on top of the covers, staring at the ceiling. As tired as she was, she couldn't seem to fall asleep. Her thoughts were going around and around and every time she closed her eyes, she saw Jack's face. And then there was the calf. Eden was worried about her.

After an hour of lying there she got up, put on some sandals and went downstairs. When she walked out the front door, she could hear the others still around the corner on the veranda, talking. Gathering up the hem of her nightgown, Eden walked quickly across the property to the barn. A dim light shone from an electric lantern hanging at the far end. A man Eden hadn't met yet sat in a chair tilted so far back it was in danger of toppling over, with his feet resting against the wall and his hat down over his eyes. The calf was lying where she'd left it earlier; its eyes were closed.

"Excuse me," she said softly, trying not the startle the man.

His chair came down abruptly and he snapped his hat back on his head.

"I'm Eden Sloane." She kneeled next to the calf and rubbed its head. "How's she doing?"

"Still hasn't eaten anything."

She looked over her shoulder at the man. "You can leave if you want. I'll stay here with her for the rest of the night."

"Are you sure you want to do that?"

"I'm sure."

"Well, all right then. If you need anything, sing out. Someone'll hear you."

"Thank you. Where's the glove?"

He pointed to a large bucket that contained melting ice. The glove, a rubber band twisted around the top to keep the milk from spilling, lay on top.

Eden reached over and picked up the glove before settling onto the straw and putting the calf's head in her nightgowned lap. All was quiet as the man's footsteps faded away. "Okay, baby. Let's give it another try." She rubbed the finger against the calf's mouth. "Come on. You can do it."

The calf looked up at her, unafraid this time, but otherwise didn't respond.

Quick tears sprang to Eden's eyes. "Please," she said softly, "if you don't drink some of this, you're going to die." She did her best to tempt the calf for the next few minutes but finally gave up and put the glove back on the ice. "We'll try again in a little while." With the calf's head still on her lap, Eden lay back against the hay with a sigh and at last closed her eyes.

When Jack walked into the barn half an hour later, he found her sleeping quietly. Without disturbing her, he pulled a chair into a darkened corner and sat on it, content just to watch. Her breasts rose and fell with each breath, gently moving the soft cotton of her gown. Her hair, some of it caught beneath her and some of it fanned out around her, shone in the lantern light like sunny silk. His eyes moved over Eden's lovely face and the soft pulse at the vulnerable base of her throat.

She stirred, and the sound of her body moving against the hay drifted gently through the air. Her eyes slowly opened and she lay there for a moment staring at the ceiling. Sitting up carefully so as not to disturb the calf, she reached for the glove and tried once again to coax her into drinking. "Come on," she murmured. "Just one lick. Do it for me." She moved the glove against the calf's mouth. "Do you have any idea how pretty you are?" Eden asked as she stroked her face. "And those eyelashes. I have friends who would kill for eyelashes that long."

There was no reaction.

Eden sighed. "I don't know what else to do. Don't you want to live?"

Suddenly the calf's long tongue sneaked its way out of her mouth and licked off the milk left behind by the trailing glove. Eden's heart moved into her throat. "That's it, sweetheart. Try it again. Just a little more. Come on."

The calf bumped its mouth against the glove and suddenly took the finger into its mouth and started sucking. Eden kept stroking her head encouragingly.

"Oh, that's a girl. That's a good girl. I knew you could do it. You're going to be fine."

The calf stopped before the glove was empty, but it was a start. Very gently she lowered the calf's head from her lap. "We'll try again in an hour," she said as she put the glove back on the ice. "I'll be right back. I want to tell Jack."

Jack moved out of the shadows. "I'm here, Eden."

She turned to him, her face alight with happiness. "Did you see? She took the milk."

"I saw. Congratulations."

Eden threw her arms around his neck and felt his arms go around her. When she realised what she'd done, she loosened her grip and moved back a little so she could look up at him, suddenly ill at ease. "Thank you for bringing her here. I know it wasn't exactly what you would have normally done."

Jack pushed her long hair away from her face. "And in this case I would have been wrong."

Eden's mouth parted softly as she looked up at him. She wanted to run, but her feet wouldn't move.

Jack's thumb followed the curve of her jaw, then gently rubbed against her mouth. With his eyes looking into hers, he slowly lowered his head until their lips met. It was a soft kiss, gently exploring. His fingers tangled in her hair as he cupped the back of her head, drawing her closer to him. He lifted her slender body into his arms and walked the few feet to where she'd been sleeping earlier. Lowering her onto the sweet-smelling hay, he lay next to her, his long body stretched out, and pulled her yielding form against his.

Their faces were inches apart as they gazed at each other in the dim light. Eden ran her fingers through his thick hair, delighting in the feel of it, while Jack stroked the smooth skin of her cheek. "I have wanted you," he said in a whisper as his mouth moved softly against hers, "since the first moment I saw you."

"This isn't right." Her voice didn't sound convincing, even to her own ears.

"Nothing has ever been more right. We've been building up to this since New York."

"Jack..."

Jack pulled her mouth back to his and shifted his body so that Eden was on top of him, her long hair hanging like a curtain around them. She could feel his heart beating through the thin cotton of her nightgown and wondered if he could feel hers. His hands moved down her back, cupping her rounded bottom, holding her tightly against him.

Emotions she'd never felt before surged through Eden. Her control was slipping. She wanted him every bit as much as he wanted her. "No!" Eden almost screamed as she pushed herself off him and jumped to her feet. She dragged shaking fingers through her hair and pushed it away from her distressed face.

Jack got to his feet and started toward her. "Eden, I—"

"Please, don't touch me."

His arm dropped to his side. "What's wrong?" he asked quietly.

She put her hand over her pounding heart. "I'm engaged. I can't do this."

Jack shook his head, not knowing what to make of the panicked woman in front of him. "It's more than that."

She didn't say anything.

"Eden, talk to me."

"I don't want to talk to you. I don't want to be touched by you. I don't want anything to do with you. Just leave me alone." She turned and ran from the barn all the way back to the house, not stopping until she was safely in her room with the door closed behind. Without turning on the light, relying on the moonlight shining through the open windows, Eden sat on the edge of her bed and picked up the telephone. If she could just talk to Richard, everything would be fine.

No. She slammed the phone down and paced back and forth, finally ending up on the window seat with her arms wrapped around her legs and her chin resting on her knees. Her throat tightened and a hot tear rolled down her cheek. What was wrong with her?

Jack stood unmoving for a full five minutes, trying to figure out what had just happened. Shaking his head, he bent down to gently touch the calf. "I'll be right back."

As he walked to the house, the moonlight tracking his steps, he looked up at Eden's dark window and paused, then went onto the veranda and walked around to where he still heard voices. Beth looked up at him and smiled. He walked to where she was sitting and leaned over her shoulder. "Can we talk?"

"Of course."

"Privately."

She touched David's hand, and he paused in his conversation with Terry and Jillie. "I'll be right back," she whispered.

Jack walked with her around to a darkened part of the veranda and waved her into a chair while he leaned against the railing. "How long have you known Eden?"

"It seems like forever," she said with a smile. "But I'd have to say that we really became close when we were about ten."

"Tell me about her."

Beth looked at him curiously. "She's a complicated subject. What do you want to know?"

He looked thoughtfully into the distance and then turned his attention back to Beth. "Why is she so afraid of me?"

"I didn't realise she was."

Jack shook his head. "Oh, Beth, you should have seen her. We kissed, and she came as close to panic as I've ever seen anyone."

Understanding dawned in Beth's eyes. "All right. Now I understand."

"Well, help me."

"I hope I can in a way that makes sense." She considered her words. "You see, Eden has been more or less on her own since she was born. Her parents were very social—still are—and I think for them her birth was an unfortunate accident. She was placed in the hands of some servants and forgotten while her parents got back to their travelling. They've never been there for her at any of the important moments of her life. Not Christmas, birthdays, graduations. Not even when she had an almost fatal car accident five years ago. They sent presents and the best doctors money could buy, but she could never count on them. The result, in my opinion and that of my analyst, is that she's taught herself not to need anyone else. If anyone gets too close to her, she builds a wall. A lot of people take it for aloofness. I've always seen it for what it is, which is fear. Fear of making a connection with another person that could end in rejection or desertion.''

Jack tiredly scraped his fingers through his hair. ''I had no idea. I must have scared the hell out of her.''

''Eden has always been rigidly controlled. I've never known her to let anyone break that façade.''

''What about Richard?''

''He hasn't even scratched the surface.''

''Why would she agree to marry him?''

''Because he's nice and nonthreatening. He takes her at face value and doesn't probe at the emotions bubbling beneath her surface. She's safe with him, and she won't have to be alone any more.'' Beth eyed the man across from her. ''And she obviously doesn't feel safe with you.''

''I would never do anything to hurt her.''

''She doesn't know that.''

''And she never will if she leaves here after the wedding.''

''Then we have to come up with a way to make her stay.''

Jack sighed. ''She's supposed to be your best friend. Why would you be interested in steering her away from Richard and towards me?''

''Because I saw the way she looked at you tonight,'' Beth said softly. ''I've never seen her look at anyone like that. You've tapped into her vulnerability. Now all you have to do is try to take things more slowly with her.''

''Time is a problem.''

''We'll think of something.''

Jack's mouth suddenly curved. ''I've got it.''

''What?''

''I know how to keep her here, but I'll need your help.''

''I'm willing.''

''Good. The first thing we have to do is . . .''

CHAPTER FIVE

"EDEN!"

Eden came running down the hall and into Beth's room. "Here I am. It took me a minute to find the flowers for your hair."

Beth clutched Eden's arm. "No matter what, don't leave me again."

Eden smiled at her friend. "A little nervous, are we?"

"Nervous? I'm terrified!"

"There's no need to feel that way. You're marrying a wonderful man."

"Oh, I know, I know. I don't understand why I'm feeling like this."

"Because you're a perfectly normal human being."

"Human, maybe. Normal, never." Beth dropped Eden's arm and tugged at her unruly curls. "And I can't do anything with my stupid hair."

Eden put a hand on her friend's shoulder and gently pressed her onto a stool in front of the mirror. "How do you want the flowers arranged?"

"I don't care. Do it any way you want."

Eden picked up a brush from the dresser and ran it through Beth's hair, pulling it on top of her head and holding the curls in place with decorative combs. Then she took the sprays of baby's breath and arranged it among the curls. "There," Eden said as she stood back to admire her handiwork. "What do you think?"

"I think I'm going to faint."

Eden laughed and hugged her friend. "Oh, Beth, you're about to start a whole new life with the man you love. Nothing could be more wonderful than that."

Beth smiled suddenly and exhaled a long breath. "You're right. I was being silly. Now I'm going to be calm." She took a deep breath, closed her eyes and once again slowly exhaled. "There. That's much better."

Eden counted to herself. Five, four, three, two—

Beth suddenly shot off the stool. "The ring! Where's David's ring? Eden, I've lost it!"

Eden picked up the thick gold band from the dressing table and handed it to her.

Beth put her hand over her pounding heart and sank back onto the stool. "I can't take this much longer."

Strains of music drifted to Eden's ears. "You won't have to. That's your cue."

Beth's wide eyes met Eden's. "This is it."

"Are you ready?"

"As ready as I'll ever be."

Eden looked into her friend's eyes and then hugged her. "Beth, you're going to be so happy."

There was a loud knock on the door and Beth jumped. "Who's that?"

"It's me, Bethie," came Terry's voice. "It's time to get going here."

Suddenly Beth grinned at Eden. "Wait until my father meets Terry and finds out I asked him to stand in Dad's place to give me away. He'll have a stroke."

Eden laughed, then grew more serious as she looked at her friend. Beth was wearing a long white dress with rushes of lace at the high neck and ends of the long sleeves. She wore no veil and that was somehow appropriate. "Beth," she said softly with a catch in her voice, "you look exquisite."

Beth hugged Eden tightly. Both women knew that, however much they tried to keep it the same, their relationship was about to change forever. Then she stepped away and straightened her shoulders. "All right. I'm ready. Let Terry in."

Eden walked to the door and opened it. Terry looked her over and emitted a low whistle, then turned his attention to his sister-in-law-to-be. "Okay, Bethie. Getting a bit toey, are you? Last chance to back out and marry the right brother."

Eden smiled as she walked out the door to the head of the staircase. She stayed there, gazing down at the seventy-or-so guests seated on either side of an aisle that had been created by the arrangement of the chairs. David, looking dashing in his dinner-jacket, stood in front of the minister. To his right was Jack, tall, straight and strong, also in a dinner-jacket.

Jack. She'd done a masterful job of avoiding him over the past couple of days. Now if she could just get through this evening, everything would be fine. Tomorrow she was headed home to the safety of New York and Richard.

At the proper moment in the music, she began her descent. Jack turned and his eyes went straight to Eden. Her bare shoulders rose out of an emerald satin dress. The top of the dress was closely fitted to just below her hips and then flared out to the middle of her knee. Her golden hair was drawn softly away from her face and caught with a clip whose length was outlined by a delicate posy. Loose curls cascaded down her back to her waist. For Jack, at that moment, no one else existed. She literally took his breath away.

Eden walked down the aisle, vividly aware of Jack's gaze. She didn't want to look at him, but something outside herself compelled her eyes to rise to his as she took her place opposite him. From that moment on, everything was a blur for her. She was vaguely aware of Beth coming down the aisle and standing beside David. The words of the ceremony reached her ears as a soft buzz. All the while Beth and David were becoming man and wife, Eden was remembering the way it had felt to kiss Jack; to feel his body, warm and hard against hers.

She automatically moved beside Jack to follow the newlyweds down the aisle. They were immediately converged on by the guests, all of whom were happy about the marriage and ready to celebrate.

All of the doors were thrown open to let in the warm night air. Barbecues were fired and mounds of shrimp, skewers of marinated beef, vegetables and lobsters were tossed on. Local musicians played some rousing music and the party was on. Most of the partygoers ended up moving between the house and the attractively lit front yard. Champagne and beer flowed freely, with beer turning out to be the odds-on favourite.

Eden watched in fascination. These hardworking men and women partied with the single-mindedness of people who were afraid they'd never go to another party as long as they lived—and they were having a wonderful time.

She'd lost Jack in the initial rush of people and found herself moving among the guests and laughing in a carefree way she couldn't remember ever doing before. More times than she could count Eden was swept into the arms of a friendly rancher and whirled around until she was breathless. One of them twirled her straight through the garden and into Jack's arms.

He held her close as he gazed at her flushed face. "Having fun, Eden?"

She was determined not to react the way she had before and forced herself to relax. "It's the best party I've been to in a long time."

The tempo of the music slowed and their bodies gently swayed together.

"There's no reason for you to be afraid of me, Eden. I would never do anything to hurt you."

Eden looked at him in genuine surprise. "Me? Afraid of you? I don't know why you'd think that."

"It might have something to do with the way you ran away from me the other night and the way you've avoided me ever since."

"That has nothing to do with fear. I simply prefer not to be in your company."

"I thought we were getting along well."

Eden stopped dancing as her eyes looked into his. "We were," she said softly. "Too well. Excuse me, but I really have to talk to Beth about something."

Jack watched her walk away.

Jillie moved into the arms that Eden had vacated. "You haven't danced with me all evening."

Jack smiled at her, but his heart wasn't in it.

Terry caught Eden by the arm as she hurried past him. "Hey, beautiful, where are you off to?"

"I don't really know."

He looked at her and knew instinctively not to joke. "Come on," he said as he looped her arm through his. "Let's the two of us go for a little walk."

Automatically they headed for the barn where the calf was, Eden's high heels leaving light stabs in the moonlit dust of the road.

Terry glanced down at her. "You want to tell me what's wrong?"

"No."

"That's honest."

When they entered the barn Eden went straight to the calf, who was doing much better by now and even standing on her own. Terry watched her for several minutes. "You do cluck over that one, don't you?"

Eden smiled as she scratched the calf's nose. "If someone would have told me last week that I'd be feeling this way about a calf, I wouldn't have believed him."

"It does stretch the limits of credulity."

She looked at him over her shoulder. "Perhaps I should have asked what's bothering *you*."

"Me? Nothin'. I'm a shallow sort."

"I don't think you're nearly as shallow as you'd like everyone to believe."

"Don't bet on it." He knelt next to her and scratched the calf behind the ears. "Eden, how do you go about making someone fall in love with you?"

A wry smile curved her mouth. "Boy, are you asking the wrong person."

"You're getting married to that Richard fellow. How can you be the wrong person?"

"Let's just say I haven't had a lot of experience at love. Or should I say in love?"

"I know what you mean." He sighed. "What's it feel like to love someone?"

"I imagine everyone has a different experience."

"Probably. Tell me this, then. How can you tell the difference between infatuation and real love?"

"Oh," she said softly. "I would imagine that real love makes you feel warm all over. You want to be with that person just to be with him, because without him there's an emptiness that nothing else can fill."

"Is that how you feel all the way out here without your Richard?"

"Richard?" she asked with a smile. "What happened to good old 'Dickie?'"

Terry grinned suddenly. "Carn, that really annoyed the hell out of him, didn't it?" His smile faded suddenly as he looked at her over the head of the calf.

"You did a neat job of not answering my question. My compliments."

"You want honesty?"

"Yeah, I do, Eden."

"All right. No, that's not how I feel when I'm not with Richard."

"Then why are you marrying him?"

"Because I don't think either of us is destined for a grand passion. The two of us have a lot in common, and we're very comfortable together."

"That's it?"

"That's all I need."

"Far be it from me to judge someone else, but it seems to me you're not asking enough out of life."

Eden removed the glove from the ice bucket and held it up for the calf. "We all view things differently. Besides, how did we get onto the subject of my love life? I thought we were talking about yours? Who's the lady in question?"

"Jillie."

"She's lovely."

"She's all of that. Doesn't take me seriously, though."

"I thought she was interested in Jack."

He nodded. "She was, but I think she's given up on him as a lost cause. He sees her as a sister. Nothing more and nothing less. Personally, I can't see that changing at this late date."

"Have you told her how you feel?"

Terry shook his head. "I'm not into that kind of rejection."

"You won't know until you try."

"That's true. Thing is, though, that this way, in limbo as it were, there's still hope. Once she rejects me, that's it."

"What are you going to do?"

"I thought maybe you could help me out there. If you were Jillie, what would you want?"

The glove finger slipped from the calf's mouth. Eden held it up again so she could grasp it. "I suppose I'd like some sign of tenderness. Maybe less flip humour. Perhaps some sign of a bit more maturity."

"Oh, that was really below the belt."

"You asked."

"I did that." He leaned over suddenly and kissed her cheek. "Thanks, Eden."

She put the glove back in the bucket of ice. "You're welcome. I think we should get back to the party."

"You don't want to talk about yourself?"

"No."

"I'm a good listener."

She looped her arm through his. "I'm sure you are, but I'm fine, really."

Terry was unconvinced but dropped the subject.

As soon as they arrived at the noisy house, Beth crossed the living room and hugged her. "I'm so glad you're here to share this day with me."

"I wouldn't have missed it."

"Listen," Beth said in a lower voice. "Jack told me that you wanted to buy Savato for my wedding present, but that he wouldn't sell him. I love that horse. Thank you for the thought."

Jack walked over at that moment. "Did I hear my name being taken in vain?"

"Kind of. Why won't you sell Savato to Eden?" Beth asked.

"Because he isn't for sale." He looked at Eden as though he'd suddenly got an idea. "However, I'll give him away."

Eden looked at him suspiciously. "Give him away? What are you talking about?"

"A little wager."

"What kind of wager?"

"If you can last here on the station for two weeks, I'll give you the horse, which you, in turn, can give to Beth and David as a wedding present."

Eden was all set to turn him down. The last thing she wanted to do was spend more time here than was absolutely necessary. But Beth suddenly shrieked and threw her arms around Eden's neck. "Oh, Eden, please. I really want that horse."

"Beth, I—"

"Two weeks is nothing when you think about what's at the end of it."

"I have things to do in New York. My own wedding needs to be planned."

Beth's face fell. "Of course. It was selfish of me to even ask you to do something like that."

Eden relented. She couldn't stand to disappoint Beth. Surely she could get through two more weeks in Australia—and two more weeks with Jack Travers. "All right, all right. I'll stay."

Again Beth threw her arms around Eden. "I knew you wouldn't let me down. Thank you."

"You're welcome." She sounded considerably less enthusiastic than Beth.

Terry walked over to them, a beer in his hand. "I'm back, friends." He handed the beer to his brother. "Excuse me, but I'm going to take a turn with Ms. Sloane here."

Eden's eyes met Jack's, then she looked away. She didn't even want to think about the next two weeks.

With great ceremony, Terry led her through the gate to an area of the yard where other couples were dancing and pulled her lightly into his arms.

"You seem to be my designated rescuer this evening."

"I'm honoured by the role."

"What's going on with you?" she asked suddenly. "You certainly have been speaking clearly lately."

"What do you mean?"

"I've understood every word you've uttered this evening. When you were in New York, I needed an Australian slang dictionary to get me through a conversation."

Terry grinned at her. "I think I'm tired tonight. I don't feel like pulling anyone's leg."

She looked at him more closely. "Terry, are you sure you're all right?"

"Yeah. Just a little depressed. I'll get over it. I always do."

"You should be dancing with Jillie."

"I should be dancing with you. You looked as though you needed a friend."

"I do. I wish you'd come a few minutes earlier, though."

"What are you talking about?"

"Five minutes ago I had my arm twisted into spending another two weeks here."

"How?"

"If I stay, Beth gets Savato."

Terry's eyes widened. "You can't be serious! Jack would never part with that horse."

"Apparently he will—for a price."

"And you agreed to it?"

"I didn't have a lot of choice."

"If that's what our little Bethie was squealing over, I suppose you didn't." He thought about it for a moment. "Well, there are worse things. You might even get to liking life on a cattle station."

Eden already liked it. That wasn't the problem.

Terry looked down at her, his eyes full of sympathy she couldn't see. If Jack had made up his mind that he wanted her, Eden didn't stand a chance.

"Let's drop this dignified trot and boogie!"

Beth looked up at Jack. "I told you my idea was better than yours."

"It definitely worked."

"For a man who just got what he wanted, you don't look very happy about it."

"I hate to trap her like that."

"As we both know, it's either that or say goodbye to her altogether."

"The end justifies the means?"

"In this instance it does. I love her, too, you know. I would never do something like this if I didn't think it was in her best interest."

Jack watched Eden dancing with his brother. He'd never been more sure of anything in his life than he was about his feelings for Eden Sloane.

"Oh, Beth. Two short weeks."

"That's two weeks you didn't have before."

He nodded, his eyes never leaving the two dancers.

Beth gently touched his arm. "What is it? What's wrong?"

Jack was silent for a moment, as though trying to find the words. "Has there ever been something you desperately wanted, and when you finally had it in your grasp, all you could do was watch it slip through your fingers?"

"Yes," she said quietly. "As a matter of fact I know exactly what you're talking about."

"I don't think I've ever felt quite so helpless. How do you go about making someone feel a security in another human being that they've never experienced before? How do you make a person feel a kind of love they've never felt before and don't understand?"

"Maybe you can't," she suggested. "Maybe you just have to turn away."

Jack shook his head. "That's not one of the options."

"Then you go after her until she's yours and don't ever let her go."

"Here." He handed her the beer. "Hold this for Terry, will you? I'm going for a walk."

Beth's gaze followed him into the distance as far as the moonlight would allow. Then she turned her eyes on Eden. David walked up to her and put his arm around her waist. "Why the sad expression?"

She leaned her head on his shoulder. "I just wish everyone could be as happy as we are."

As they watched, another man tapped Terry on the shoulder and began dancing with Eden. Terry made his way over to Beth and David and reclaimed his beer. "Thanks. Where's Jack?"

"He went for a walk."

"Seems to be a popular pastime this evening." He took a long drink. "I understand the two of you and Jack manipulated Eden into staying an extra two weeks."

"Manipulated?" Beth asked defensively.

"What would you call it?"

"I'd call it doing what's right for my friend."

"Whether it's what she wants or not."

"Eden doesn't know what she wants."

"She seems to think she does."

It was dawn when the guests finally started to make their way home. Eden went upstairs to the sound of cars starting and goodbyes being shouted. After washing her face, brushing out her hair and slipping into her nightgown, she perched on the window seat and stared outside. The last car pulled away and disappeared into the dusty sunrise. After a long silence there was a noise—as if someone had left the house. She leaned slightly forward and saw Jack walking down the steps and into the yard, already dressed for work. He couldn't possibly have got any sleep.

She watched until he was out of sight, then closed the drapes and climbed beneath her soft, clean-smelling sheets, only to lie there with her eyes wide open and focused on the dark ceiling. Always in the past she'd been so sure of herself. That changed the day Jack Travers walked into her life. Nothing was certain any more.

Eden sighed and rolled onto her side, wrapping her arms around a pillow and hugging it close. Two more weeks. That was all she had to get through. Then everything would return to normal.

Two more weeks with a man called Travers. She could handle it. Just because she was attracted to him didn't mean she had to do something about it. She'd kept her distance from people all her life. There was no reason to think she couldn't do it with Jack.

Feeling a little better, Eden slowly closed her eyes and fell into a restless sleep.

CHAPTER SIX

EDEN spent so much time tossing and turning that she finally gave up. Mrs. Cleary had washed the clothes she'd borrowed from her granddaughter and brought them back to Eden, and that was what Eden put on. Pulling her hair back into a free-swinging ponytail, she grabbed her hat and went downstairs. The mess from the party had already been cleared away. She went into the kitchen and found the housekeeper washing the last of the dishes. "Good morning."

Mrs. Cleary turned to her with a smile. "Good morning, dear. You're up awfully early."

"I couldn't sleep."

"It was exciting, wasn't it? That's the first wedding we've had around here for years and years. It was long overdue, too, if you ask me. Young people these days wait forever to get married."

"They don't want to make a mistake."

"I suppose. But in my day, things were very different, I can tell you. Can I get you some breakfast?"

"Just some juice. I can get it myself."

Mrs. Cleary shook her head and looked at Eden's slender figure. "You really need to eat more."

Eden poured herself a glass of juice and put the container back into the refrigerator. "I can pack it away at times."

"Humph."

"Has Jack had breakfast yet?" she asked casually. A little too casually.

"I don't know. I slept a bit later than usual this morning."

Jack walked in at that moment. The back of his shirt already stuck to his damp skin. As he took off his hat and tossed it onto the counter, he looked at Eden in surprise. "What are you doing up this early?"

"She couldn't sleep," Mrs. Cleary answered for her. "Where've you been?"

"Checking some things. We're going to start moving the cattle today."

"Where to?" the housekeeper asked.

"The north range."

"That's a long haul."

"I know, but it has to be done."

Eden took a long drink of her juice. "Would you like me to help?"

Jack lifted an expressive brow. "You want to help with a cattle drive?"

"Why not?"

"Well, it's not quite what you're used to."

"Nothing here is what I'm used to."

"It's fine with me, but are you sure you want to do this?"

"I'm positive. I really can't see myself sitting around the house for the next two weeks."

"All right. We need all the help we can get. Thank you. You're going to end up earning that horse."

Mrs. Cleary looked from one to the other and smiled.

"Are Beth and David still sleeping?" Jack asked as he turned away from Eden.

"I assume so," the housekeeper answered.

"You'd better get them up. Chris Dooley is going to be here soon to take them to Sydney so they can catch their plane to France. If they miss one, they're going to miss the other."

Mrs. Cleary wiped her hands on a dish towel. "I'll do that right now."

When she'd gone Jack poured himself a glass of cold water and sat at the counter across from Eden. His blue eyes roamed leisurely over her face. The faint shadows under her eyes told him more clearly than words what kind of night she'd passed.

Eden had to tell herself once again that he was only a man. She had nothing to be nervous about.

"I checked on your calf this morning. She's doing really well. I think we'll be able to let her run with the rest of the herd in a month or two."

"Even without a mother?"

"Now that she's gotten some strength back, maybe we can find someone to adopt her."

"Do cattle do that?"

"They're very generous animals."

Eden grew silent as she stared out a window, unaware of the way Jack's gaze softened as it rested on her. "I assume I'll need to pack some things...."

"Don't worry about it. I'll have Mrs. Cleary get some clothes ready for you."

"Thanks."

"I should warn you that this drive is going to be unrelentingly hot, dusty and tiring."

She turned her gaze to his. A faint smile touched her mouth. "Good. I'm not in the mood to be comfortable."

"Then you've definitely come to the right place." He finished his water and walked over to the sink to set his glass down. "I have some work to finish around here, and I know you want to say goodbye to Beth. We'll head out as soon as they've gone."

"All right. I'll be ready." Her eyes followed him out the door. There. That hadn't been so hard. If anything, it would probably get easier over the next two weeks. Then Beth would have her horse, and she could go home and take up her life.

Eden heard someone come into the kitchen and turned to find Beth, bleary-eyed but awake, standing there squinting as her eyes adjusted to the bright light of the kitchen. "Tell me it's not really morning," she moaned.

"It's not really morning," Eden said obligingly.

"Nice try." Beth winced and put her hand to her head. "I think I overdid the champagne."

"You're allowed on your wedding."

"That's fine, but I forgot I was going to have to pay for it today." She walked over to a cupboard and took out a bottle of aspirin from which she removed three, and swallowed them quickly with a glass of water. "I hope these things take effect before we have to get on the plane."

"What time are you going?"

"Twenty minutes from now."

"Are you packed?"

Beth nodded as she sat across from Eden. "We did that yesterday before the wedding." She suddenly smiled. "I can't believe I'm actually married."

"Do you feel different?"

"You mean from when I was single? Absolutely. And it's a wonderful difference. Imagine wanting to spend the rest of your life with someone." She sounded in awe of the very idea. "It's kind of an amazing thing."

Eden smiled affectionately at her friend. "You look happier than I've ever seen you."

"Oh, I am." Beth looked at her watch and groaned. "Fifteen minutes. I'd better make sure my husband is out of the shower and dressed." Again she smiled. "My husband." With a little shake of her head, she left the kitchen.

Eden finished her juice and walked out to the veranda to sit on the swing. It was a beautiful morning, bright and cheerful, with just a hint of the heat to come. As she sat there, gently propelling herself to-and-fro, she realised for the first time how much she genuinely liked it here. Several men on horseback rode past the house, laughing loudly at something.

Her ears picked up the sound of a plane in the distance, approaching the station. Within minutes it came into sight as it circled over the house and then landed on the cleared strip near Jack's plane.

She heard David and Beth struggling with their luggage long before she saw them. "What did you pack anyway, Beth?" he asked. "Bricks?"

"Of course. I always pack bricks when I'm going on a long trip. Honestly, David. I only put in the bare necessities."

"Bare necessities my eye," he muttered. "We're staying for three weeks, not three years."

"You'll regret your attitude when you see how gorgeous I'm going to look."

Just as they walked out the door, Jack pulled up in a Jeep. "Come on, you two."

David looked over at Eden. "Morning." Then he turned his attention back to his wife. "I'm telling you, Beth, if you ever pack this much again, you're going to be carrying your own luggage. I'm a man, not a mule."

Beth went up on her toes and kissed his cheek. For a moment they smiled at each other. Then he went on to the Jeep, and Beth walked over to Eden. "Come on to the plane with us."

The two women walked to the Jeep arm in arm. Eden got in the front with Jack while Beth climbed into the back with David. It took only a couple of minutes to drive down the track to the waiting plane and pilot. Jack helped David load the luggage while Beth and Eden watched. Then Beth turned to her friend and hugged her. "You take care of yourself."

"You, too. Have a wonderful time."

"I intend to." Beth started to go to the plane, but stopped suddenly and turned back. "Eden, I love you. You're my sister in every way that's important, and more than anything else I want you to be happy. You know that, don't you?"

"I know."

"Then try. If not for your sake, then for mine."

Eden started to say that she was happy, but the words never came. Jack stood next to her as Beth and David got on the plane, and it comforted Eden to have him there with her as they taxied and turned, then sped down the field and lifted into the air. Shielding her eyes from the sun with her hand, she waved for a moment, then stood still and watched until they had almost disappeared from sight.

"Are you all right?" Jack asked quietly.

Eden lowered her gaze to his. "I'm fine. Just feeling a little lost."

"You still have me."

A smile curved her mouth, delighting the man. "Is that supposed to make me feel better."

"Yes."

She looked at him for a long moment. "What now?"

He returned her look, then took her arm as they walked back to the Jeep. "We pick up your things from Mrs. Cleary and head out to the herd."

When they pulled up in front of the house, Mrs. Cleary was sweeping off the veranda. "I'll be right back," Jack told Eden as he went into the yard and quickly up the steps. He came out a moment later with two backpacks, set her hat on her head and nodded towards the stables. "Let's go."

Eden adjusted the chin strap of the hat as she fell into step beside him, wondering exactly what she'd gotten herself into.

"Are you ready for this?" he asked.

"Strangely enough, I'm looking forward to it. Of course," she qualified, "you realise my anticipation stems from complete ignorance."

Jack laughed.

When they got to the stables he led from her stall the same mare Eden had ridden before. She knew which saddle to use this time and automatically put it on her horse, along with the water pouches and backpack Jack handed to her. Jack gave her a boost onto the horse, then pulled himself onto his own and rode outside. Four men, one of them Les, sat astride their own horses and were waiting for them. With a minimum of greetings, they all started riding. For the most part the six rode abreast. Eden fell behind just once and nearly choked on the dust kicked up by the others. After that she kept up.

After a couple of hours they stopped to water the horses and give them a break from the heat. The men sat on the ground in whatever shade they could find in the shelter of some old gum trees, and Eden sat with them, listening to them talk. Or trying to. She could understand the words, but there was so much slang involved that she hadn't the vaguest notion what they were talking about.

Jack saw the intense concentration on her face and smiled. He was going to have to teach her how to speak Australian.

After a few minutes she wandered away and stood in the full sunlight staring into the distance. Jack came up behind her. "What are you thinking?"

She looked up at him. "Do you remember when we first met?"

He returned her look for a long moment. "Yes."

"You said something to me then about wide-open spaces."

"I remember."

"I'm beginning to understand a little of what you meant. I can't tell you when the last time was that I was in a place with no traffic and few people."

"And?"

"I think I like it."

"Even in this heat?"

"Well, I could do nicely without that, but the heat is what made this land the way it is."

"Our winters are more pleasant."

"I'm almost sorry I won't be here to experience that. I've noticed that every several miles there seem to be little shacks. Do people live in them?"

"No. They're temporary shelters for my men. With the weather we get here at times, they need a place to go."

As the other men began mounting their horses, Jack looked at Eden. "Ready?"

She nodded.

"Let's go, then."

They made several more watering stops. Every once in a while Les would start singing. He had a wonderful tenor voice that was easy on the ear. The other men, instead of joining in, just listened as they rode. Sundown wasn't too far away when they finally neared the herd.

Eden smelled the cattle before she saw them. The air was thick with the dust they'd left behind. She could feel it coating her damp skin. Her first inclination was to wipe it off, but then she realised it would be a never-ending job and she might as well get used to it. After a while, she didn't even notice it any more.

The cattle, moving slowly over the land with the stockmen beside them, stretched as far as the eye could see. Some of the men had bandannas tied around their faces to protect their mouths and noses from the dust that hung in the air like a thick fog. Jack reached into his pack and pulled one out for Eden. "You'd better put this on. You might need it."

She gratefully took it from him. "Thank you."

"I want you to stay close to me at least for today, and probably tomorrow, until you've gotten a little used to things."

"All right." She had to shout above the noise as she tied the ends of the bandanna together behind her head.

"Come on."

She followed him at a fairly fast clip to the front of the herd, which, as it turned out, did indeed have a beginning and an end. The man in charge looked at her in surprise, doffed his stained hat, and then promptly ignored her while he talked with Jack.

Eden moved slightly away from them and watched in fascination as the herd moved with slow deliberation, almost as one animal. Everything was calm and organised. One steer strayed away from the main body and a stockman was there immediately, riding beside it, coaxing it back to the herd.

"Come on, Eden," Jack called to her as he rode around the front of the herd and back down the other side. She followed, stopping when he stopped, blinking against the dust.

She spotted a steer that had moved out of the herd and automatically rode after it, the way she'd seen someone do earlier. Moving her horse the way he had, she gently nudged it back into the herd.

Jack stopped talking and watched her, then turned back to the man, a smile behind his eyes, as he finished his conversation.

Eden, immeasurably pleased with herself, brought her horse up alongside Jack's and waited. As soon as he'd finished, he turned his horse and sat facing her. "You catch on fast."

She pulled the bandanna from her face and let it rest on her neck. "It's kind of fun."

"Think you could get used to this kind of life?"

"I could definitely get used to Australia. Cattle drives are something else. I'd like to do this maybe once every five years. Or ten."

"There aren't very many women who participate at all."

"Now you tell me! Why am I here?"

"Because you asked to be."

"Ah. And you didn't warn me."

"That's right."

She smiled suddenly. "Thanks. Where do we go now?"

"Around to the rear. Pull up your bandanna."

Eden did as he asked and followed him down the line of moving cattle.

Suddenly there was a thumping noise in the air. Eden looked up and saw a helicopter making its way towards them.

"There he is," Jack said as he stopped to watch.

"Who?"

"Terry."

"Why is he in a helicopter?"

"It comes in handy on cattle drives."

Terry flew in closer and lower, whipping dust from the dry earth into a choking frenzy, then retreating and landing some distance behind the herd.

Eden, coughing, tossed Jack a dry look as he laughed. "I take it that was done for my benefit?"

"I think that's Terry's way of telling you g'day.'"

"Remind me to say hello back in an appropriate way the next time an occasion presents itself."

"I'd like to see that."

"I'll invite you." The two of them trotted their horses to the helicopter and got there just as Terry climbed out.

"G'day, you two. How's the dust?"

"Thicker than it used to be," Eden said with a twinkle in her eyes.

"No fooling." He glanced at his brother. "How'd she take my entrance?"

"Let's just say that I wouldn't turn my back on the woman for the next two weeks if I were you. What took you so long?"

"So long? I was moving flat out like a lizard drinking. Short of flying a Concorde, I couldn't have gotten here any sooner." He took his hat off and wiped his bare forearm across his forehead. "Jeez, it's hot today, isn't it?"

"Yeah," Jack agreed as he leaned forward in his saddle. "Worse than usual."

"What do you suppose it is?"

"I don't know. It could mean some kind of storm."

They looked concerned and Eden didn't understand it. "Wouldn't that be good?"

"It all depends on what kind of storm," Jack explained. "In the kind we get out here, it doesn't always rain. Then again, sometimes it does rain and the ground is too hard to absorb it, so we end up with floods." He turned his attention back to Terry. "Did you get the fuel leak on the truck fixed?"

"Sure did. That little beauty'll run on the smell of an oily rag now. Should be along in a few hours with the rest of the supplies."

"Thanks for taking care of that."

"No probs. Where's my horse?"

"By the water truck. I think what we're going to do now is get the stock close to Roddy Creek, or at least what's left of it, and bed them down for the night."

"Right. I'll get saddled up and join you."

Eden found herself staring at Jack's profile as he squinted against the bright sun falling lower in the sky.

He seemed to have forgotten she was there as he gazed thoughtfully into the distance. There was something about this man that was solid and secure. Aside from being physically attracted to him, Eden was finding that she liked him.

Jack turned his head at that moment and their eyes met. "Come on."

Eden followed him back around the herd. The men got the animals to veer slightly north and started slowing down the pace. By the time sundown arrived Roddy Creek was in sight and the cattle made straight for it. The stockmen sat astride their horses and patiently watched as the thirsty cattle drank their fill, then led them across the creek to bed down for the night.

"How do you watch the cattle at night?" Eden asked as she splashed her horse through the shallow creek with Jack.

"In shifts mostly, so that all the men get at least a few hours' sleep."

"You included?"

"Me included." He smiled at her. "You, however, will be allowed to sleep the night through."

"I accept."

"I thought you might. How are your legs holding up?"

"Surprisingly well. I'm not nearly as sore as I was the first time out. Of course, I haven't touched the ground yet, either."

They rode to where a kind of camp was being set up. Trucks, some with food and some with water, had parked in a wide circle. The food truck had already been unloaded and kerosene stoves were being used to cook two huge kettles of what smelled like stew.

"I thought the cooking would be done over a camp fire," she remarked to Jack as they took their horses behind the trucks and tethered them to a line that had been strung.

"Not these days. Things are so dry around here that you can't even drop a cigarette butt without worrying about the consequences." He turned to a young man who didn't look a day over eighteen, skinny as a stick with a hat a size too large. Eden hadn't seen him before. "Joey, make sure all the horses are watered, fed and brushed down. They don't like the dust any more than we do."

"Yes, sir."

Men trickled in one by one until the camp buzzed with conversation and laughter. Jack stopped to talk with one of the men. Eden stood there for a minute, but the fellow looked as though she made him nervous as he stumbled over his words and shifted from one foot to the other. After a few minutes she politely excused herself and walked over to Terry. On the way across the camp though, she noticed that the men were looking at her kind of sideways and grew quiet as she passed. When she got to Terry, who was sitting with his back against a truck tyre and drinking a cup of water, she sat next to him—or rather *sank* onto the ground next to him—and pushed off her hat to hang down her back. "May I ask you something, Terry?"

He smiled at her. "Anything, gorgeous."

"I thought you Australians were all gregarious. Why does everyone get so quiet when I walk by?"

"You're with the boss. They're merely being respectful."

"I hate to think I'm killing their fun."

"Don't worry about it. They'll loosen up when they get to know you a little better. I did."

"As I recall, you were already quite loose when we met."

He grinned. "True."

The sun was nearly down. All that remained was a burst of orange in the distance. Battery-powered lanterns were placed at intervals around the camp. Eden's eyes went to Jack, who was still talking—or rather listening. His hat was in his hand. He bent over and used it to knock some dust from his jeans, all the while reacting to what was being said. As though he sensed her gaze, Jack looked up and into her eyes. Eden wanted to look away but couldn't. What was it about him that drew her so?

Jack walked over and hunkered down in front of her. "As soon as it gets completely dark we'll set up an area where you can wash the dirt off."

"I can just do what everyone else does."

"No, you can't," he said with a half smile. "Trust me on this one."

"What do the others do?" she asked suspiciously.

"They either don't wash at all until the end of the drive—figuring they'll only get dirty again in the morning—or they sponge off here in camp in front of God and everyone."

"Oh. You're right. I can't do that." She looked around and didn't see any tents. "Where does everyone sleep?"

"On blankets."

"On the ground?"

"That's the general idea."

"Under the stars, so to speak."

"Exactly. It's beautiful out here at night. The sky's incredibly clear."

She nodded. "Another new experience."

"Are you about 'new experienced' out?"

"Not yet. But then I've only been at this for one day. Talk to me tomorrow night."

Jack suddenly smiled at her. "You're a lot more relaxed today than you have been."

"I noticed that as well," Terry said.

"I'm going to be here for two weeks. Being tense that long would be exhausting."

"So you're taking the easy way out."

Her eyes met Jack's. "On the contrary."

The muscle in Jack's jaw tightened suddenly. "Eden Sloane, when this drive is over, the two of us are going to talk."

Eden knew what he meant. There was no mistaking the way he looked at her. She could feel his desire across a room. "It won't make any difference," she said quietly.

"We'll see." He got to his feet. "I'll check on that bath area for you."

Terry took another drink of water. "He's in love with you, you know."

Eden looked at Terry and then out at the camp. "He wants to sleep with me," she told him with surprising bluntness. "There's a difference."

Terry shook his head. "You're reading him all wrong. I know Jack better than anyone else on earth. He's different with you."

Eden looked at him curiously. "Different how?"

"Protective. Gentle. Patient."

"You can see all that?"

"I'm more observant than I'm given credit for." Terry looked at her for the first time since he'd started talking. "Eden, don't blind yourself to what's happening because you feel some kind of obligation to that Richard character. You're engaged to him, not married. I have to admit that, when I first figured out what was going on, I warned Jack away from you. Or at least I tried to. But the better I've gotten to know you and the more I see the two of you together, the more I think Jack knows what he's doing. There's something between you I've never seen before."

Eden didn't say anything.

"And on that note," he said as he got to his feet, "I'm going to have some dinner. Can I bring you back a plate?"

"No thanks. I'll get it myself."

"Mad at me?"

A smile touched her eyes. "No. I just think I should mingle with the men a little."

"Good idea."

Eden sat quietly for a few minutes, then rose to join the line of men that had formed. Some of them smiled rather shyly at her and she smiled back. When she got her plate of stew, she looked around for a place to eat and spotted a group of men sitting in a half circle, laughing about something. Jack was suddenly at her elbow. "Come on. I'll take you over."

"Do I look nervous?"

"Only to me. They won't bite."

And they didn't. She and Jack sat cross-legged on the ground. Jack joined in the conversation, and Eden listened as she ate, fascinated. Apparently her fascination showed, because the men soon relaxed and returned to their easy bantering, though they made an effort to clean up their language. When one of them slipped he'd promptly apologise to Eden. She gave up telling them it wasn't necessary.

When dinner was over she and Jack took their plates back to the truck, and the men began breaking into smaller groups, some of them bedding down for a short night, some talking quietly. Les sang a sad, quiet song in that wonderful voice of his. The notes seemed to linger in the air long after they were sung.

Jack took Eden to where a blanket had been strung between a gum tree and a truck. ''There's a tub of warm water, soap, towels and whatever else you might need there.''

''Thank you.''

''Take your time.'' He indicated a blanket on the ground. ''You'll be sleeping there.''

''All right.'' She went behind the hanging blanket and quickly stripped out of her dusty clothes. The ''tub'' wasn't big enough to hold a person, but held more than enough water to do a good job. The first thing she did was dunk her head in to get the dust out of her hair. Shampoo from her backpack had been laid out and she used it sparingly, lathered, then dunked again to rinse. Soaking a washcloth, Eden soaped it and scrubbed her skin until it glowed, then rinsed by scooping water out of the tub and letting it run over her skin. Using a towel, she quickly dried herself off and dressed in the clean clothes for tomorrow, which she found in the backpack that Jack had provided. Her brush was in there, too, and she took it along with her backpack when she went to her bed and sat on her blanket, pulling it through the quickly drying strands in long strokes. Jack, lying on the ground a few feet away, his head pillowed on his arm, watched. And Eden was intensely aware that he was watching.

Lanterns all around the camp had been dimmed; voices that had been talking and laughing were now quiet. The cattle, so close by and so noisy when they were moving, were still except for the occasional "moo."

Eden set her brush down and lay back on her blanket, pulling another one over her. After a moment she slid her backpack under her head to use as a pillow. The sky was pitch-black, and against that backdrop the clarity of the stars was something to behold. She'd never seen anything like it. One of the stars seemed to move quickly across the sky, and she watched it in surprise.

"That's a satellite," Jack said quietly as though he knew exactly what she was thinking.

"Oh."

"You sound disappointed."

"I thought it was a falling star."

"And if it had been, what would you have wished for, Eden?"

"Peace of mind, I think. I don't seem to have had much of it lately." She turned her head and met his gaze through the darkness. "Goodnight, Jack."

"Night, Eden."

CHAPTER SEVEN

EDEN rode to the front of the herd where Terry was and pulled her horse alongside his as they rode. "How's it going, girl?" he called to her.

"Just fine. I can't believe I've already been out here five days."

"I have to give you credit, Eden. I thought you'd have given up a long time ago."

"I'm nothing if not tenacious. Are you going back with Jack and me today?"

He shook his head. "I'm going to hang out here for a while with the stockmen and make sure the herd gets settled in."

Jack rode up beside them and looked across Eden to his brother. "Hey, Terry, have you noticed that the herd seems a bit edgy today?"

Terry nodded. "I did notice. I think it might be the weather. The air's a lot heavier today than it has been. It's been kind of building since the first day we got out here."

"Well, keep an eye out. It won't take much to spook the fellows."

"I'll be watching."

Jack turned to Eden. "You come with me and stay close. I don't like the feel of things around here today."

Feeling a little spooked herself, Eden followed him down the line of the herd. Things went along smoothly for the next half-hour, though it was obvious that all the men were more alert than usual. The herd's jumpiness had affected everyone.

Suddenly there was a loud report. Eden jumped and looked around, trying to locate the source. It could have been anything from a gunshot to a dead limb snapping away from one of the gum trees.

The herd suddenly came alive—almost as though that was what it had been waiting for. Eden had never seen anything like it. The animals surged forward like an enormous tidal wave and began a blind run that threatened to crush anything in its path. Her heart in her throat, Eden look frantically around for Jack, but he was gone and she was sitting on a horse that had begun to rear in nervousness. Dust rose up and covered them both in a cloud as thousands of panicked hooves thundered by.

Eden saw the other stockmen riding fast to keep up with the herd, trying to make sure they stayed on a straight path. There wasn't much else they could do. Wheeling her horse around, Eden kneed her mare and started running with them, hoping that the mare would expend enough nervous energy to make her more controllable.

The stockmen's efforts to keep the chaos organised were futile. As soon as the front lines veered to the left, the others blindly followed. Eden saw a stream of them separate from the main body and quickly rode after them to steer them back to the herd.

She never got there. The little mare shied suddenly at something on the ground that looked like a snake. She reared violently, her front legs going straight up in the air. Eden tried to hold on but couldn't. She felt her grip loosening on the reins and felt herself falling through the air. Before she'd even hit the ground, the little mare took off without her.

Eden got up quickly, then stood almost frozen as the main body of the herd shifted direction towards her. There was nowhere to run. Without realising what she was doing, she screamed Jack's name and suddenly he was there, scooping her onto the back of his horse while still at a dead run, just seconds before the herd trampled over the ground where she'd been standing. Eden wrapped her arms around his waist and clung tightly, her face buried in his back. She could feel the hard muscles of his stomach through her fingertips as he maintained tight control over his horse. As quickly as that she stopped being frightened. She knew she was safe as long as she was with him.

Somehow, after more than ten minutes of the herd's kamikaze run, the stockmen managed to get the animals turned slightly and running in the direction they wanted them to. After another five minutes the cattle began slowing and the stockmen regained the control the herd had wrested from them.

Jack rode Eden to the back of the herd near the water truck and gently lowered her to the ground. "Stay here. I'll send someone to look for your horse. And put your hat up."

Eden obediently lifted her hat from her back, where it had fallen, to her head, and tightened the chin strap as she watched him ride away.

The driver climbed out of the water truck and handed her a cup. "Never a dull moment, eh?"

"Thank you." She took a long drink and got some of the dust out of her mouth. "What happens next?"

"They pretty much make sure the herd is well and truly calm. Some of the men will fan out to look for strays. I noticed from back here that a good chunk of stock broke away from the main herd and headed into the scrub."

"Was anyone hurt?"

"Not that I know of. We were lucky this time. We aren't always."

Eden took another drink and handed him back the cup, then sat on the bumper of the truck to watch and wait.

The herd moved ahead while the trucks stayed behind. She hadn't seen Terry at all and was beginning to wonder where he was when she heard the helicopter. It didn't come near the herd but stayed to the far sides and seemed to be looking for strays. If it hovered in one place, some stockmen would head in that direction.

When Jack came back almost two hours later, he had her horse in tow. Eden took the lead rein in her hand and checked her over. "Is she all right?"

"A little thirsty but otherwise fine. As soon as you get her something to drink, we'll take off."

She looked at him in surprise. "We're leaving?"

"The herd's within a few miles of the final destination, and I think they're too hot and too tired to do
any more running."

"What about the strays?"

"We've gotten a good number of them back.
Between now and tomorrow I'm sure they'll have the
rest."

Eden gently rubbed the mare's nose. "I'll get her
watered and collect my things."

"All right. Don't take too long. As it is, we won't be
making it all the way back home today."

Eden walked her mare around to the rear of the
water truck and the alert driver handed her a bucket.
The mare drank nearly half of it before she was satis-
fied. Then Eden got her gear from one of the other
supply trucks and rode the mare to where Jack was
waiting. Without saying anything, the two of them
rode off, their horses keeping a steady pace that
wouldn't drain them in the heat.

Jack seemed quiet and distant. Whenever Eden tried
to start a conversation, he'd give her a monosyllabic
answer. She finally gave up and rode silently beside
him. Towards evening there was a light breeze. It was
heaven after the still heat, and Eden raised her face
and let it wash over her.

When the sun started to set Jack stopped riding and
looked at the horizon. His mouth tightened. "Bloody
hell," he swore under his breath.

Eden looked at the sunset also. It looked fine to her.
"What's wrong?"

"Do you see how the sunset looks dulled?"

Eden narrowed her eyes and looked more closely. "Yes. It's almost like we're looking at it through gauze."

"It's not gauze. It's dust."

"Dust?"

"The weather's been heading for this all week. I knew something was going to happen. I just wasn't sure what."

"I still don't know what you're talking about."

Jack's eyes met hers. "Have you ever been in a dust storm?"

"No."

"Well, you're about to, unless we can get to a shack before it hits. There's one about an hour from here. We might just make it if we ride hard."

"But what about the stockmen and the cattle?"

"The cattle have been through these things before. They'll know enough to turn their backs and shelter among each other. The men will have seen what we see by now and will have started digging in and fastening things down. Let's get going or we're going to get caught in it. That's not one of the features of Territory life that I want you exposed to." With that, Jack kneed his horse and galloped off, and Eden quickly followed.

The breeze grew stronger and stronger until there was nothing pleasant about it any more. Particles of sand blew against Eden's face, stinging her skin. Stopping her horse for a moment, she pulled out the bandanna she'd been wearing when working with the cattle and wrapped it around her face. By the time she'd finished Jack was so far ahead of her she had to race to catch up and then only succeeded because he noticed that she'd fallen behind, stopped and waited.

"Keep your head down," he called to her. "Let your hat take the brunt of it. Just make sure you keep your eyes on my horse's tail so you don't get lost. We have at least another fifteen minutes."

As they raced off, Eden did exactly as he'd said, riding slightly behind him, her head down, her narrowed eyes on his horse. The wind grew even stronger, slowing them to half the pace they wanted because the horses were having a hard time pushing against the wind. It was like riding constantly uphill. The tiny granules of sand being whipped along in the hurricane-like winds penetrated the thin material of Eden's blouse. The wind caught her hat and blew it off her head. She grabbed at her chin strap and jammed the hat back on.

Jack leaned low over his horse so that his body was no longer a foil for the wind. Eden did the same. When they finally got to the shelter, Jack jumped from his horse and caught Eden at the waist to help her down. As soon as she was on her feet the wind caught her light form and blew her to the ground. Jack picked her up in his arms, kicked open the door of the shack and stumbled in with her. He was holding the reins of the two horses and they followed them in. As soon as Jack put Eden down, he slammed the door shut and bolted it. It was pitch-black and hot. "Feel around for some kind of torch," he told her as he moved the horses to a corner and tethered them.

"Torch?"

"Lantern. There's one here somewhere."

Eden groped in the dark along the bare wood walls until she came to a small cupboard. Her searching fingers found canned food but not much else. She moved her hands along a dusty counter until at last she found what she was looking for. With a flip of the switch, they had a dim light. The battery had obviously seen better days because the light flickered uncertainly. It would only be a matter of time before that was gone.

While Jack unsaddled the nervous and exhausted horses, Eden took off her hat and bandanna and looked around. The shack had the bare minimum of comforts, but to Eden, at the moment, it was beautiful. In addition to the food, there was also a good supply of bottled water. She poured some into a bucket she found in the corner and gave it to first one horse and then the other.

Jack sat on the floor and leaned tiredly against the wall. When Eden had finished with the horses, she drank some water herself, straight from the bottle, and handed it to Jack as she sat next to him. The wind howled all around them, ferocious in its intensity. It was as though it were trying to wrench the small structure from its very foundation and carry it along with it. The sound of the sand blasting against the corrugated tin roof was eerie and deafening.

And then there was Jack.

During the past several days with him she'd felt a certain calm. There were the wide open spaces, a huge herd of cattle and nearly two dozen men around at all times. But now they were in a cramped little shack, and it was just the two of them. She couldn't have been more aware of him if he'd been touching her.

The lantern flickered for an instant and went out, but just as quickly came back on, its dim light barely illuminating the corner it was sitting in.

"Are you hungry?" he asked.

"No."

"Then maybe we should just lie down and get some sleep." He reached out and touched her hand. "You're very quiet. Are you all right?"

Eden pulled her hand away from him and jumped to her feet. "I'm fine. Just fine."

Jack watched her curiously. She didn't sound fine at all. Her words had come out so fast they'd almost tumbled over each other.

She walked over to the cupboard where the food was and stood staring at it without really seeing it. Her fingers drummed nervously on the counter. God, she wished that wind would stop.

"Eden," Jack said quietly—yet still loudly enough to be heard over the wind, "relax. We're inside and we're safe."

"I know. I am relaxed," she lied. "I'm fine." She started pacing back and forth.

"This will be over within a few hours, and at first daylight we'll be out of here and on our way again."

She nodded, but still she paced. Her heart was racing faster and faster as if to keep up with the wind. The walls seemed to be closing in on her, pushing her towards Jack. Eden's chest tightened. It was difficult to breathe. She needed to get away from him. More than anything else in the world at that moment, she had to get away. Racing suddenly for the door, she threw back the bolt and yanked it open, running outside into the wind. The first gust nearly knocked her over, but she regained her balance and tried to run on.

Jack caught her from behind. He hauled her protesting form into his arms and tossed her over his shoulder to carry her back inside. As soon as he had the door bolted closed again, he set her on the floor. Taking her shoulders in his hands, he gave her a good shake, his own breath now coming in winded gasps. "Eden, snap out of it. What the hell's wrong with you?"

Eden felt tears well in her eyes and cursed herself for her lack of control. "I can't do this any more. I just can't."

"Do what? What are you talking about?"

"This. Being here with you and acting like it doesn't matter. I can't pretend any longer."

Jack gazed into her eyes, his own expression growing tender. "Oh, Eden, you never had to pretend with me. I knew better anyway." His mouth came down on hers, gently at first, searching, but as he felt her instant and passionate response, all of his good intentions disappeared.

Eden wrapped her arms around his neck, tangling her fingers in his thick hair. Still kissing, they both sank to their knees. She let go of years of pent-up emotion in that moment. Her control had snapped and she didn't care. She wanted this man more than she'd ever wanted anything in her life. She needed to feel him against her, around her, inside her; as close as two people could get.

She wanted to touch his skin, but his shirt was in the way. Without even realising what she was doing, she ripped at it and the buttons scattered on the floor. Still kneeling, Jack pulled her close as Eden's hands moved inside his shirt, over his muscled stomach and around to his back, pulling him tightly against her.

Jack groaned as she moved against him. "Eden, we can't do this. Not here. Not this way."

She kissed her way down his strong, tanned throat to his chest, her mouth becoming gentle and seeking.

Jack suddenly grabbed her by the shoulders and held her away from him. "No, Eden, no. Don't."

She gazed at him, her eyes filled with surprise and hurt. "I don't understand."

Jack rose and walked away from her as he dragged shaking fingers through his hair. "I'm not sure I do, either. God only knows that this is what I've wanted from the moment I laid eyes on you in New York." He turned back to her and went down on his knees in front of her, cupping her dusty, lovely face in his hands. "Eden," he said softly. "I don't just want to make love to you. I want to spend the rest of my life with you."

"You want to marry me?"

"More than I've ever wanted anything in my life."

"Why?"

"Because you're my destiny. Don't you feel it, too?"

"I've been too busy trying to avoid you to feel anything but threatened."

He shook his head. "Oh, Eden, the time we've wasted."

"Oh, no!" she suddenly whispered.

"What is it?"

"Richard. I can't do this to him."

"What you can't do is marry a man you don't love. That kind of sacrifice won't do either of you any good."

"I know you're right. But this isn't something I can tell him on the phone. I'll have to go back to New York and tell him in person. I owe him that much."

"I'll go with you."

"No," she said softly. "This is something I really have to do alone."

"We'll talk about that later." Jack walked over to the saddles and removed the blankets that were rolled up and attached. After spreading them out on the floor, he lay down and held out his arms for Eden.

She lay next to him, her head on his shoulder. The lantern flickered for a final time and died, leaving them cozily in the dark. Jack pulled Eden closer and sighed contentedly against her hair. "I love you."

"I love you, too," she said in wonder.

Suddenly there was a loud crack outside, and thunder rolled through the air. Eden lifted her head. "It's raining."

Jack got up, went to the door and opened it. The wind had died down a little. "It's not raining."

"But the thunder . . ."

"It's just an electrical storm."

Eden moved next to him and Jack put his arm around her. The two of them watched as lightning forked across the sky. Even as they stood there, the dust storm died down even further.

"Out of one maelstrom and into another," he said quietly.

Eden looked up at his profile etched against the darkness. "What do you mean?"

"The electrical storm doesn't look like much, but when things have been this dry, there's no telling what it can set off. A couple of years ago something like this started a fire and burned out entire towns." He watched the lightning, deep in thought. "Eden," he finally said, "I know how tired you must be, but I want to try to get home tonight."

"All right."

"I can't explain it, but I have a feeling that I should be there."

"We'll go right now."

In the darkness they saddled their horses and led them outside. The wind was still strong, but the dust was less biting. Eden fastened her hat onto her head and pulled the chin strap tight. Then they mounted and started on their eight-hour journey.

Lightning sliced the night sky. The air was filled with a loud crack as a bolt struck a tree not fifty yards away, slicing it cleanly down the middle. It burst instantly into flames from top to bottom.

Jack stopped his horse and pointed into the distance. "Look at that."

Eden saw a line of fire on a low hill miles away, glowing orange in the black night. In the space of minutes the wind had spread it.

"I hope I haven't gotten us into something I can't get us out of. Come on. We don't have any time to waste. Don't fall back. Stay up with me as best you can. If it becomes a problem, let me know and we'll slow our pace."

They rode hard for two hours, then had to stop because of the horses. Eden felt sorry for them. Not only was it hot, it was humid. The wind brought no relief because of the dust.

They stopped in the open rather than near trees because of the lightning. Jack dismounted, then helped Eden. As he lowered her to the ground, he gently kissed her. "I guess you realise already that by marrying me, you aren't exactly walking into an easy life."

Eden reached up and touched his mouth lightly with her fingertip. "I don't care. In fact, I'm looking forward to it. We can build our world together."

Still holding their horses's reins, they sat on the ground close to each other. More lightning forked through the sky, and the horizon was still on fire. But where they were, in the middle of nowhere, sitting in the open with the wind washing over them, there was a strange peace.

"I was thinking," Eden said.

"About what?"

"Maybe instead of going home with you, I should go back to the herd and get some men," she replied.

"It's a nice thought, but too risky."

"I have a good sense of direction."

She felt his smile through the darkness. "I'm sure you do, but this isn't like a city with streets where I can tell you where to turn. You have to know where you're going. It's hard for anyone to find after only having been there once. There's nothing more dangerous than getting lost out here."

"But what's going to happen if you get home and find out you need them?"

"That probably isn't going to happen, but I'll tell you this right now, Eden. I'd rather lose everything I own than risk something happening to you."

Eden reached over and took Jack's hand in hers. She held it close to her and rubbed her cheek against it. "Right now, with things the way they are between us, I find myself wondering why I ever fought my feelings for you."

"Beth thinks she knows."

"Beth?"

"She and I had a long talk."

"Did your talk have something to do with a certain horse named Savato?"

Jack squeezed her hand. "Actually, that little bet was Beth's idea. I'll have to thank her for that next time I see her."

"Me, too," Eden said quietly.

"I don't ever want you to be afraid of your feelings for me. They can't be any more intense than what I feel for you. I'll always be there for you."

"I know." She rested her head on his shoulder. "I honestly do know that."

Jack kissed her hair. "Let's get going again."

They stopped only one more time to water the horses. It was daybreak when they came within sight of the station. Black acrid smoke rose from one of the buildings, but since they were still some distance away, it was impossible to tell which building was burning.

CHAPTER EIGHT

THEY raced the remaining miles to the station as fast as the exhausted horses would allow. When they got into the yard a scene of utter chaos greeted them. More than a dozen neighbours who had come to the rescue surrounded the stables in a long line, passing buckets full of water and tossing the liquid into the flames. It was a futile effort.

Jack leaped off his horse and ran to the man at the hand pump who was drawing the water. "Bill, we should be using the hoses."

Bill inclined his head towards the storage shed—what was left of it. Now it was just a blackened shed. "No hoses. And the generators are out. None of the pumps are working. It's either do it by hand or don't do it at all."

"Stand back!" someone yelled.

Before Eden's horrified eyes, the roof of the stables collapsed from the centre outwards, leaving a great, gaping hole of flame. In a matter of minutes the walls collapsed in on each other. The stables were gone.

The wind was whipping the flames into a frenzy, picking them up and actually blowing them across the yard. Some of them landed on the barn. The dry wood that had sat baking serenely in the sun for years went up like a tinderbox.

The calf!

Eden jumped off her horse and raced with the others to the barn. As she was about to run in, Jack grabbed her arm. "No."

"But the calf might still be in there."

"I'll get her. You wait here."

Eden waited as long as she could and then ran in after him.

"Dammit, Eden," Jack said as he bent over the piteously mooing calf, "I told you to wait outside."

"I can help."

"You'll get yourself killed. Just get out."

"I'm not going to leave you in here."

The calf was terrified and wouldn't budge. Jack finally had to pick it up in his arms. "Then we'll both get out. Come on."

The barn was already filling up with thick smoke. Only a few feet behind them a burning beam crashed to the ground. Jack handed the calf to one of his station hands. "Find a safe place for this." Then he turned back to the business of trying to save what he could by starting a second bucket brigade. Eden joined him. For what seemed like hours in the hot, relentless sun with the flames of the fire adding its heat and the smoke blackening their skin and clothes, they stood there passing bucket after heavy bucket of water. Eden's arms and shoulders ached with the effort, but all she had to do was look at Jack's determined expression and she was able to keep going.

Mrs. Cleary had prepared a mountain of food for the growing crowd of fire fighters. A few here and a few there took short breaks to rest and eat, then started again.

Jack finally gave in to the inevitable and yelled, ''No more! It's no use.''

Eden stood beside him. He put his arm around her and together they watched the last of the barn disintegrate into flames. The wooden legs of a cylindrical storage tank next to the barn collapsed and the metal tank hit the ground with a hollow thunk. A tall tree next to the barn caught fire. Eden could hear the pop of the sap inside as it burned. Within minutes it started to fall—almost in slow motion. Everyone backed away as it hit the ground, showering everything in a fifty-foot radius with burning debris. The wooden fence of the corral where Savato had been was the next thing to catch. Soon the corral was surrounded by a ring of fire. There was another storage shed in definite danger, but when the others would have damped it down with their buckets of water, Jack told them to leave it alone. ''We have to wet down the house. It's getting too close.''

The line reformed. This time Eden manned the pump, pulling it up and pushing it down so that a steady stream of water gushed out. The trough beneath it didn't have a chance to fill up because of the people dipping in their buckets. They started with the roof and the veranda. Blessedly, the sun began to set.

A man came to relieve Eden at the pump, and she immediately picked up a bucket. Another tree, this one near the house, shot up in flames. The wind caught some of them and carried them to the roof. People began shouting and racing out of the line with their buckets to douse whatever fire they could. Steam rose from the wet roof, but the flames were persistent and quickly dried out what had taken hours to dampen. Fire moved from the roof and down a pillar to the veranda. In minutes the railing was on fire and moved from there to the veranda itself. While some men raced in and out of the house to rescue furniture, others stayed outside to battle the fire. Eden watched in horror as the tenacious flames got a stranglehold on the house that couldn't be broken by their meagre buckets of water.

With a final streak of lightning and crack of thunder, the rain began. But it was too late for the house. Everyone stopped working and just stood still, exhausted, as the rain poured over their soot-streaked faces. Eden walked over to Jack and took his hand in both of hers. "I'm so sorry," she whispered.

Beyond words, he just shook his head as he watched the flickering flames hissing in the rain.

One of the men walked over to Jack and put his hand on his shoulder. "You're welcome to spend the night at my place."

"Thanks, Bill. For everything. I think I'll stay here tonight. The supply shed is still standing. I'll bunk in there. If you don't mind, though, I'd like Eden and Mrs. Cleary to go with you."

"That's fine. Mollie will be happy to have them."

"No."

Jack looked down at Eden in the light of the dying flames. "I think it's best, Eden."

"I want to stay with you."

"There's nothing left here."

"It doesn't matter. Nothing matters except that we're both safe and we're together."

He cupped her face in his hands and kissed her forehead. "All right. I guess Eden and I won't be taking you up on your offer, Bill, but I'd still appreciate it if you'd see to Mrs. Cleary."

"Right." Bill patted Jack's shoulder again and joined the others as they drifted away from the house to where they'd parked their cars some distance away, safe from the fire.

When the last of the cars had pulled away, Jack took Eden by the hand. "Come on. Let's go."

"But the house, Jack..." Flames still licked the now-wet veranda.

"My watching it isn't going to make it any better. I'm tired. I just want to get some sleep so tomorrow I can go over things and calculate the damage."

Hand in hand they trudged over the muddy ground to the small supply shed some one hundred yards past what remained of the barn. Once inside Jack tried the light switch, but nothing happened. He groped through the darkness and found a lantern. When he turned it on the shed came to life. Stacked on shelves were blankets, clothes, canned foods, sleeping bags, lanterns, flashlights, hats. Anything the men might need was there.

Jack dug through the clothes for a moment until he found what he wanted, then handed Eden a shirt and some trousers. "We'd better get out of these wet clothes. Towel yourself down with a blanket and slip into these."

Eden walked around to the back of some free-standing shelves, took off her soggy shirt and trousers and vigorously rubbed her skin with the soft blanket until it was dry, then did the same thing to her wet hair. She raked it back from her face with her fingers and used the same band she'd had on earlier to catch it in a damp ponytail.

The shirt Jack had given her was long. The tails came to just above her knees. She didn't even bother with the trousers but set them aside for tomorrow.

When she walked back around the shelves, she saw that Jack had been doing the same thing as she and was now in dry trousers and an unbuttoned shirt. He took two sleeping bags from one of the shelves and laid them out on the floor next to each other. After turning out the lantern he pulled Eden down with him. His arm circled around her. She rested her cheek on his shoulder, desperately wishing there was something she could do to take away the pain she knew he was feeling.

But they were safe. Safe from the fire and safe from the rain that now slashed against the window of the shed.

She reached across Jack to a low shelf, pulled off a blanket and draped it over the two of them, then lay back, her cheek against his shoulder, her hand resting lightly on his solid stomach.

Jack kissed the top of her head and sighed.

Eden started to say something.

"Don't," Jack said softly. "Let's just lie here quietly. I don't want to talk. I don't even want to think right now." He pulled her closer. "I just want to lie here with you in my arms."

As exhausted as Eden was, she couldn't sleep. She kept hearing the rain, and in her mind's eye, she kept seeing the fire. She was still shocked by the utter devastation.

"Eden?" Jack said softly after a long silence. "Stop thinking and get some sleep. You're going to need all your strength for tomorrow and so am I."

"Promise that you'll sleep, too?"

"I promise."

When Eden awoke the next morning, she was alone on the sleeping bags. Bleary-eyed, she rose up on her elbows. "Jack?"

When there was no answer she quickly got up and put on the trousers Jack had given her the night before, along with her battered shoes, and walked out the door. A beautiful, bright morning greeted her, giving no hint of the weather's fury the day before. As she stepped onto the ground, her feet immediately sank into a quagmire of mud left behind by the rain. When she tried to walk one of her shoes got sucked off her foot. She finally gave up trying to keep her shoes on at all and just left them behind so that she could squelch barefoot through the mud to the house.

Parts of it were still standing, though the roof seemed to have been almost completely burned off. All that was left of the veranda were some blackened boards and gaping holes where fire had destroyed the wood altogether. Eden walked through the completely destroyed garden and saw Jack standing in the doorway. He reached out a helping hand and pulled her up into what had once been the lovely foyer. It was now nothing more than a sooty shell. The staircase she'd so admired the first time she saw it was still standing, though it was burned almost beyond recognition.

"Careful where you step," Jack warned her as they started through the house.

The kitchen was almost intact, but there was heavy smoke damage. As they moved throughout the rest of the house, what became clear to Eden was that there wasn't an inch of space in the house that didn't need some work done to it. And major work was necessary in at least half of the house before anyone could inhabit it.

Jack suddenly turned Eden into his arms and held her tightly. "Oh, Eden. When I asked you to marry me, I did it with such high hopes. Now I have nothing to offer you."

Eden pulled away from him and looked into his eyes. "I love you, not this place. We can build this back up together. We can do it."

He looked around the foyer and shook his head. "I think I should just tear the whole thing down and start over again."

"I'd hate to see you have to do that," she said softly. "The lines of this home are so beautiful. Maybe you can get a structural engineer in here to look it over and see what needs to be demolished and what can be saved."

"Perhaps you're right."

Both of them heard the helicopter at the same time. Jack went to where the front door had once been and watched Terry as he slowly walked through the yard, looking around with a disbelieving expression in his eyes. "My God," he whispered hoarsely.

Jack gave him a hand up into the house.

Terry looked his brother in the eye. "I've got more bad news."

Jack said nothing. He just waited for the next blow.

"It's the herd. The rains hit hard out there. There was a flash flood. We lost at least half of them."

Jack dragged his fingers through his hair. "Was anyone hurt?"

"No. The men were all accounted for." Terry shook his head. "I'm sorry, Jack. We did the best we could."

Jack touched his brother's shoulder and looked outside. "I know," he said quietly.

"Where do we go from here?"

Eden watched and listened from where she stood.

"I don't know," Jack finally said. "None of the buildings were insured."

"Why on earth not?" Eden gasped.

"Because of where we are," Jack explained. "Insurance companies don't want to touch us. Natural disasters are a common part of life out here."

"What about a loan?" Terry asked.

"I'd hate to do that, but it's beginning to look like my only option. I'll see about getting someone in here to figure out what our costs are going to be, and then I'll start visiting banks."

"You're welcome to whatever I have," Eden said suddenly.

Jack smiled at her and the love he felt was obvious. "I can't take your money, Eden."

"Why not?"

"We're not talking about a few dollars here. We're talking about major, major money."

"But I want to help you."

Jack walked over to Eden and took her in his arms. "You are helping just by being here. But this is something I have to take care of on my own."

Both his brother and Eden watched as Jack turned and left the house. Terry shook his head. "I hate to see him go through that."

"Go through what?"

"Having to go hat in hand to banks that'll never give him any money."

"How do you know that? He's a hard worker. Surely they'll be able to see that."

"Because he went through it once before. The banks don't want to touch property out here any more than the insurance companies do."

"They should have more faith," she said quietly.

"You're not going to get an argument from me. But then I'm not the guy in the three-piece suit who holds the money."

Jillie drove up in her Jeep at that moment, managing somehow not to get stuck, and parked in front of the house. Long boots protected her from the mud as she walked through the pitiful remains of the garden to where Terry and Eden were standing in the doorway. "I've been in Alice this week. I just found out about the fire when I got back today. Where's Jack?"

"Somewhere about," Terry told her. "I wouldn't go after him to offer your sympathies just yet, though. I don't think he wants to hear it."

"All right," she agreed. "I'll see him another time."

"How's your place?" he asked.

"Fine. The mud's pretty bad and we lost a few head of cattle, but other than that, we didn't get hit at all." She looked at Eden with her still soot-covered face. "I take it there's nowhere to wash around here."

"The generator's down," Eden explained. "There are no pumps."

"Well, you might as well come back to my house with me. We can get you cleaned up and suited in some clothes that fit." She looked down at Eden's bare feet. "And some boots, too, until this mess dries out."

Eden really was tired of the dirt. "Thank you, Jillie. I'd appreciate it." She turned to Terry. "If Jack's looking for me, tell him I'll be back shortly."

Terry nodded absently as he started to walk through the house. "That's fine, Eden. The mess'll still be here when you get back. I'll try to do a little work on the generator to see if we can't get something going.''

Eden jumped to the ground and followed Jillie to the Jeep. She got in and watched quietly as Jillie skillfully manoeuvred the car through the mud and down the road. Her place was about twenty-five miles away, and it didn't take them long to get there. Her house was a lot different from Jack's. It was more of a barnlike structure and didn't have the same warm personality. But at least it was there, and most importantly, it was still standing.

Jillie led Eden inside and took her upstairs to a small bedroom with an attached bath. ''You go on in and shower, and I'll find you some clothes. We're about the same size.''

As soon as Jillie left, Eden stepped out of her clothes and into the shower, lavishly soaping her body and hair to get off the dust and soot. There was a blow-dryer on the counter and Eden used it. When she walked back into the bedroom, she found a pair of jeans and a white blouse, along with some socks and boots already there. Everything fitted perfectly.

Then she went downstairs to find Jillie. As she walked through the house, though, it was Jillie who found her. ''Come on, Eden. I had the cook fix a sandwich for you. It's in the kitchen.''

Eden followed her into a bright, sunny room and saw the sandwich sitting on the table.

''I know food is the last thing on your mind at this point,'' Jillie told her, ''but my guess is that you haven't had anything since yesterday.''

"I haven't. But neither has Jack."

"I figured as much, so I had Cook fix some more sandwiches for you to take back."

"Thank you, Jillie," Eden said gratefully.

The two women sat at the table. Jillie watched Eden as she ate. "You love him, don't you?"

Eden looked up at her. "Yes," she said simply.

Jillie sighed. "I don't have to ask how Jack feels about you. It's been obvious to everyone since the day you got here."

Eden finished the last bite of her sandwich, then scooted her chair back. "I appreciate your help, but right now I need to go back."

Jillie nodded. "All right. I'll get the sandwiches, and we'll be off."

The sun was high in the sky as they drove back, already drying out the mud. Jillie dropped Eden off in front of the house and handed her the bag of sandwiches as Eden climbed out of the Jeep. "If you need anything, call."

"We will. And thanks again."

Jack came walking out of the house as the Jeep disappeared into the distance. "Was that Jillie?"

Eden held up the bag of sandwiches. "She let me clean myself up at her house, and she sent these over for you."

"Oh, that's great. I'll have to thank her the next time I see her. Hey, Terry," he yelled. "Come on out. Food."

Terry, wiping his hands on a rag, jumped from the house to the ground and took a sandwich. "Thanks. I'm so hungry I could—"

Eden grinned and interrupted. "I know. I know. Eat a horse and chase the jockey."

"There now, you see? We Aussies aren't so hard to understand once you get the hang of it." He turned to his brother as he swallowed a mouthful of sandwich. "I got the generator working. The electricity goes on where the wires haven't melted, and the water pump for the kitchen works as well now as the one for the downstairs bathroom."

Jack sat down on a wrought-iron bench while he ate his sandwich and pulled Eden onto his knee, his hand at her waist. "We're making progress. I got the phone in the library to work and got hold of Joe Carson in Alice. He's a structural engineer," Jack explained to Eden. "Anyway, he can be out here later today, take a look around the place and tell us what the house needs to have done to it. And I've set up some bank appointments for tomorrow, so I'll be taking the plane."

"Maybe you will and maybe you won't," Terry said. "If the ground doesn't dry out considerably, you'll never get the plane out of here. You may end up having to take the helicopter."

"Would you like me to come with you?" Eden offered. She couldn't help but think about what Terry had said and knew that she didn't want Jack to be alone with his disappointment.

Jack shook his head. "Thank you, sweetheart, but no. I can do this on my own. You stay here with Terry."

Eden and Terry exchanged glances, but neither said anything. They didn't have to. Jack knew what he was in for as well as they did.

He gently deposited Eden onto her feet and rose. "I'm going to pick up Joe now. I should only be gone for a couple of hours. By tonight we'll know what to start on first."

Eden heard a noise coming from inside the house. "What's that?"

"Mrs. Cleary's already working in the kitchen, trying to get things cleaned up as best she can."

"I'll go help her." She kissed Jack on the cheek. "You be careful."

His eyes were tender as he gazed at her. "I always am. See you later."

She watched him walk away, then turned to Terry who was standing there, smiling at her. "What are you looking so smug about?" she asked good-naturedly.

"My, my," he said innocently, "how quickly things change."

Eden's smile grew. "Yes. Ain't life grand?"

Terry walked over and hugged her. "I don't know about life, but you sure are. Let's get to work."

He gave her a leg up into the house and Eden went to the kitchen. Mrs. Cleary, scrubbing brush in hand, was scouring the kitchen cabinets.

"What can I do?"

The housekeeper looked up and pushed the hair out of her eyes with the back of her hand. "How are you at scrubbing walls?"

"I suppose we'll find out in a minute. Is there another bucket?"

"In the broom cupboard over there." She pointed her brush.

When Eden had found the bucket, another brush and a sponge, Mrs. Cleary put the detergent in it for her. Then Eden filled the bucket with water and went to work. The soot was tenacious and didn't want to relinquish its hold on the creamy walls and dark wood. But Eden was more determined than the soot, and it eventually gave way. Side by side, the two women worked throughout the day. Eden heard the helicopter take off and heard it again when it landed. After a time men's voices came from somewhere in the house—one of them Jack's and another one she didn't recognise.

A big man walked into the kitchen. He was a redhead with a tendency toward baldness who was as tall as Jack and twice as wide. He smiled vaguely at the two working women. "I'm Joe Carson. I'll be out of your way in a minute."

As they watched, he inspected everything from the floor to the ceiling. "Jack?" he called as he scribbled on his legal pad.

Jack walked in a moment later. "Finished?"

"Yeah." The two men sat at the newly cleaned table while the engineer wrote some more. "I'll tell you," he said, "it could be worse. This section of the house is very stable, and I don't think it's going to need much work other than clean-up. The other side of the house, though, is a different story. The foyer has to be completely gutted and redone. The staircase has to be torn down and rebuilt. Three of the bedrooms upstairs have damaged walls. I don't trust them at all. They'll have to be torn down and rebuilt. And, of course, the roof is a loss. As far as the veranda goes, none of it's usable. You'll have to cart the old burned wood away and replace it with new. There are no building materials salvageable from either the barn or the stables, so those will have to be built from scratch.'' He tore the page from his notebook and handed it to Jack. ''I could be off on my estimates here, but this is what I think it's going to cost you to replace what you've lost.''

Jack exhaled sharply. ''That's three times what I paid for the buildings when I bought the place.''

''I know. It's awful the way building costs keep going up and up.''

Both men rose. Jack shook his hand. ''Thanks for coming out here. I appreciate it. I'll take you back now.''

Eden and Mrs. Cleary shared a look as the two men left. ''We've had it now,'' the housekeeper said.

Eden didn't say anything.

Almost a week later, as Eden and Terry were dragging the burned wood away from the veranda and stacking it in the yard, they heard Jack land the plane.

Eden looked up at Terry as they tossed a large board onto the pile. "I wonder what happened."

"I don't," he said grimly. "If he'd been able to cut some money loose from those banks, you can bet he would have called with the good news."

Eden knew he was right.

As they both watched, Jack drove up in the Jeep. He walked straight to Eden and looked into her eyes. "Oh, I missed you."

She put her arms around his neck and hugged him. Jack looked at his brother over Eden's shoulder and shook his head.

Terry swore softly and kicked at a piece of wood. "I knew it. I knew they wouldn't give you the time of day."

Eden stepped back, still in the circle of Jack's arms, and looked up at him. "You didn't get any money?"

"No. But it's not important. We'll just have to think of something else."

"That's it, Jack. You have no choice now," Terry told him. "It's either sell this place for whatever money you can get or go completely under."

But Eden had had the seed of an idea earlier, and now that Jack had returned empty-handed, that seed bore fruit. There was no way—no way—she was going to let him lose this place. It was too much a part of him.

Jack looked at her with a hint of a smile at the corners of his mouth, deepening the grooves in his cheeks, but she could see the pain behind his eyes. "Well, Eden, this isn't quite the life I'd envisaged for the two of us. I wanted you to stay in Australia so you could see how grand life here could be, and it's been nothing but one disaster after another.''

''I already told you that I'm adaptable.''

His slight smile faded. ''I'll understand if you want to back out.''

''No, you wouldn't,'' Eden said quietly, humour in her voice. ''You'd come after me and drag me back.''

''That's probably true. I mean, a man can't just let his destiny walk away, can he?''

''I do have to go back to New York, though. I owe it to Richard to tell him face-to-face, and I have some other personal things I need to take care of.''

''When are you leaving?''

''Tomorrow. The sooner I get there, the sooner I can come back here.''

He pulled her into his arms. ''I hate to let you go at all.''

''It'll just be for a week or two. . . .''

CHAPTER NINE

EDEN walked into her apartment, tossed her bag and keys onto the hall table and sank tiredly onto her couch. Telling Richard had been easier than she'd expected. In fact, he'd taken it almost insultingly well. A smile touched her mouth. Some days there was no pleasing her.

Her eyes came to rest on the telephone next to her. She had one more thing to do. Picking up the receiver, she dialed a number she knew well. Weston Reid had been her parents' personal lawyer ever since she could remember. She'd spoken more with him over the years than she had with her parents.

"Hello, Carol," she said when his secretary answered. "This is Eden Sloane. Is Uncle Wes in?"

"He is for you, Eden. Just a moment."

"Eden!" came a cheerful, deep voice a moment later. "I was wondering what happened to you. I called to take you to dinner last week, but you were nowhere to be found."

"I've been in Australia."

"Australia? What on earth were you doing there?"

"Falling in love mostly."

"Sounds serious."

"It is. Uncle Wes, I need to talk to my father. Do you know where he is?"

"I sure do. Your mom and dad are staying with friends of theirs in Barcelona. I can give you the number."

"Actually, I need the address. This is something that has to be discussed in person."

"Sure." He covered the phone with his hand for a moment as he called to his secretary to bring the information to him. "Anything I can help with?" he asked as he came back on the line.

"Not unless you can break my trust fund so that I can have it now instead of when I'm thirty-five."

"I'm afraid it's iron-clad, honey. I drew it up myself. Only your father can change the terms."

"That's what I thought."

"Thank you, Carol," he said. "Eden, here's where they are."

She picked up a pen from the table and scribbled down the address. "Thanks, Uncle Wes."

"Not at all."

"And I'd very much appreciate it if you don't tell them I'm coming."

"All right, all right, if that's what you want." He paused. "Eden, if you need me for anything, call."

Eden smiled suddenly. "Uncle Wes, have I ever told you that I love you?"

"As a matter of fact, you haven't," he said in surprise.

"Well, I do."

"I love you, too, Eden," he said quietly. "You're the daughter I never had. I wish we'd spent more time together over the years. Goodbye, dear. And good luck."

"Goodbye."

Eden hung up and sat there, staring at the paper she'd written the address on. Jack's future, and hers as well, hinged on what was going to happen in the next few days.

When Eden's flight landed in Barcelona, she rented a car and bought a map. Her parents' friends lived on the outskirts of town in a lovely area with wonderful estates. She easily found the one belonging to the Vilas but getting inside was another matter. A high wall and big iron gates protected the property. She leaned out of her car window and pushed a black button mounted in concrete.

A voice asked her in Spanish who she was and what her business was.

Eden dredged up as much of her high-school Spanish as she could remember.

Suddenly the guard spoke to her in accented English. "Why are you telling me that you have a cold?"

"I'm sorry. That wasn't what I meant."

"Suppose you tell me what you do mean. In English this time, please."

"I'm Eden Sloane. I understand that my parents, Kenneth and Elizabeth Sloane, are staying here. I'd like to see them if I may."

"One moment."

Eden drummed her fingers on the side-view mirror while she waited.

"Please, come in."

The gates swung in and Eden drove through them and down a long curving drive to the front of a beautiful salmon-colored mansion. A white-jacketed butler opened the arched door for her as she was walking up the steps. "I'll tell your parents you're here. Please take a seat in the music salon." He led her into a large room whose focal point was a black piano. Sunlight streamed in through the arched windows, warming the room and Eden's mood as she took a seat on the couch to wait.

No one looking at her would have guessed that the poised woman who sat there was, in fact, very nervous. Her hands were folded so tightly in her lap that her knuckles were white.

Her father walked into the room smiling, took her hands to help her to her feet and kissed her lightly on either cheek. That was his greeting to a daughter he hadn't seen in nearly three years. "What a pity you didn't call first, Eden. Your mother's out shopping with our hostess," Kenneth explained as he took a chair across from her. "So, what brings you to Spain?"

After all these years the distance between them still hurt her. But there was a difference now. She wasn't a vulnerable little girl any longer. "I have a favour to ask."

Her father waited in silence.

"You see, Father, I've been in Australia for the past few weeks. My friend Beth married an Australian and I went there for the wedding. While I was there, I became engaged to the brother of Beth's husband. His name is Jack Travers."

Her father lifted a sceptical gray brow but maintained his silence.

"He owns a cattle station," Eden explained further, sensing that she was losing her audience, "and during the past few weeks some natural and unforeseen disasters have just about wiped him out. I'm here because I want to ask you to allow me access to my trust fund so that I can help him."

Kenneth studied his dignified daughter for a long moment. "No," he said simply.

Eden blinked in surprise. She'd expected an argument, but not flat-out rejection. "Father," she said reasonably, "Grandmother and Grandfather put the thirty-five-years-old restriction onto my trust because they had no way of knowing before they died how I was going to turn out. You and I both know that I've been extremely responsible my entire life. Believe me, I'm not making this request lightly. I want the money to use towards my future and the future of the man I hope to marry."

Her father looked mildly amused. "Eden," he said patronisingly, "you're asking me to turn over to you what amounts to millions of dollars to sink into some cattle station, owned by a man you've known for just a few weeks, in some godforsaken country. I won't do it. The trust says you can't touch that money until you're thirty-five, and that's the way it's going to remain."

"Father—"

"Besides," he interrupted, "why hasn't he gotten the money from a bank if he's so desperate?"

"That's the problem. The banks won't lend him any money. Life is too unpredictable out there."

"I see."

Eden hated to beg, but she told herself that this was for Jack. "Father, please reconsider. I know what I'm doing. Jack Travers is a man who can be trusted."

"He certainly seems to have you convinced of that." He leaned back in his chair, one leg crossed over the other, his elbows resting on the arms of the chair and his hands steepled under his chin. "Tell me, Eden, what kind of life are you expecting to lead with this Travers fellow?"

"A good life. A happy life."

"In Australia?" her father asked.

"Yes."

"On a cattle station."

"That's right."

"You weren't brought up to live like that, Eden."

Eden met his gaze with a direct one of her own. Her green eyes held ice that concealed the pain of being an unwanted child. "How would you know what kind of life I was brought up to lead?" she asked with deadly quiet. "You were never there."

Kenneth Sloane looked at his daughter in undisguised shock. "Eden, don't you dare talk to me like that. Your mother and I did the best we possibly could."

The ice was replaced with unutterable sadness. "Yes, I suppose you did."

Her father decided to try reason. "Eden, this man is using you. He'll take you for every penny he can get and then leave you out in the cold. It's an old story."

Eden rose to her feet, her gaze steadily on the man across from her. "Father," she said softly, "for the first time in my life I'm loved. And I'm loved by this man." She shook her head. "I wish I could find the words to explain this to you. You see, Jack has given me the greatest gift imaginable: the gift of being able to, at long last, open my heart completely to another human being without the fear of being rejected yet again. He doesn't want my money. He wants me. But I want to come to him with all the resources at my command so that we can build a life together."

Her father rose as well. "Perhaps I could make him a personal loan."

"No, thank you. I appreciate the offer, but I don't want anything from you. Certainly not your money. This trust fund was a gift from Grandmother and

Grandfather, and that's the money I want to take to Jack. I'd appreciate your thinking it over tonight. I'll call tomorrow for your answer." She started towards the door but was stopped by her father's voice.

"Eden, I can have a room made up here for you to use if you'd like."

"No, thank you," Eden said with cool and impersonal courtesy. "I'll stay at a hotel."

He inclined his head. "As you wish."

Eden walked into the foyer, through the front door and to her car. For several moments she just sat behind the steering wheel. It had taken her twenty-five long years, but she'd finally come to terms with her relationship with her parents. At last she knew that the fact that they hadn't loved her wasn't her fault. She wasn't unlovable. They just didn't know how to love anyone but each other.

Unaware of her father's steel-grey eyes watching from inside the house, Eden started her engine and drove down the narrow driveway and out through the already opened gates.

Kenneth Sloane stared at the empty driveway long after Eden had gone. His daughter had grown into a remarkably beautiful young woman. A daughter to be proud of. But she was a stranger to him.

He turned back into the room and sat on the couch. A distant memory drifted into his mind. It was of a little girl with neatly combed, long blonde hair held away from her face with a ribbon. She was wearing a brand-new frilly dress, ankle socks and little black patent-leather shoes that her nanny had purchased for her. When her parents had walked through the door for the first time in more than a year, her green eyes had sparkled with excitement at the sight of them, and she looked as though she could hardly keep her feet still. But she was a good girl. Obedient. She knew not to run at them. Mother and Father didn't like that. And so she stood at the foot of the staircase, waiting. He remembered the way Elizabeth had walked over to Eden, leaning over to give her a cool kiss on the cheek, not even bothering to look the child in the eye. Turning to the nanny, she said, "Miss Adams, I really don't think this shade of pink looks very good on Eden. Please dress her in something more suitable," and then walked up the steps without a backward glance. And he remembered how Eden's lower lip had trembled. She'd caught it between her teeth to keep it still.

And then he remembered himself walking over to her, absent-mindedly ruffling her hair and following his wife up the stairs. There hadn't been a single hug. The next time he'd seen her was when he and his wife were on their way out the door to dine with friends. They hadn't seen their little girl in more than a year, and they hadn't even taken the time to have dinner with her on their first night home.

He was suddenly very ashamed of himself. He had no right to keep that trust fund away from her. He had no right to any say in her life at all.

* * *

Eden found a small but nice hotel not too far away, checked in and went straight to her room. For a long time she just sat on the bed. Then she picked up the phone and asked the hotel operator to connect her with Jack's phone. Maybe there'd be some good news about a loan coming through and she wouldn't have to deal with her father anymore.

Within minutes she heard the distant ringing. It rang for a long time. She was almost ready to hang up when a friendly, familiar voice answered.

"Terry," she said. "It's Eden."

"Eden! We wondered where you were. Jack's tried calling you, but you're never home."

"I've been gone a lot."

There was a pause at the other end. "Are you all right? You sound strange."

"I'm fine," she said quietly. "Can you tell me if Jack's had any luck getting money for the station?"

"None. But he did get an offer from some people to buy it, and I think he's seriously considering it. There's not much else he can do. I wish I could put him on the phone for you, Eden, but he's not here right now."

"That's all right, Terry. I'll call another time. Tell him that I . . . Never mind. Just say that I called. I'll talk to you later."

Eden hung up, and even though it wasn't yet five o'clock in the afternoon, she lay back on the bed and stared at the ceiling. All she could think about was how much Jack loved the station; the way he'd looked out at his land and welcomed her to Australia the first day she'd arrived. She couldn't bear to think of him having to sell it to strangers.

Early the next morning, Eden called her parents. Her heart was pounding, but her voice was calm as she spoke with her father. "Have you made a decision?"

There was a slight pause. "You can have your trust fund. I'll call Wes today and have it taken care of."

Eden closed her eyes and clutched the receiver in both hands. "Thank you."

"It's still going to be at least a week before you'll get the money. These things take time."

"I understand."

"Your mother was sorry to have missed you yesterday. She was hoping you might come by for lunch."

"No, thank you. I'm going back home today."

There was another pause. "Eden, I just want you to know that your mother and I—well, we wish you all the best. I hope things work out for you in Australia."

Eden felt her throat constrict. When all was said and done, she still loved her parents. "Thank you, Father."

"Goodbye, dear."

It was the first time Eden could remember her father calling her something besides her given name. "Goodbye, Father."

And with that she hung up the phone.

Exactly a week later she was at the station. The pilot she'd hired in Sydney raced his plane down the field and was in the sky before Eden had made it halfway down the track.

Terry, who'd come to the door of the house to see who'd arrived, walked down the road to meet her. Eden was so happy she dropped her suitcase to give him a hug. He grinned down at her, his arms still securely around her waist. "I don't know what the occasion is, but I like it."

"Where's Jack?"

He hugged her more tightly. "Jack who?"

"The man I'm going to marry."

"Oh. That Jack." He released her and picked up her suitcase and caught her hand in the other as they walked. "He's out in the plane, checking the rest of the stock."

"Do you know when he'll be back?"

"Any time now, I should think. He's been gone the better part of the day." He glanced at her sideways. "You want to share the news you're fairly bursting with?"

Her smile was so wide it couldn't grow any more. "I need to tell Jack first, but believe me when I say that it's something wonderful."

"I believe you, I believe you."

When they got to the house, he climbed in first then gave her a hand up. "As you can see," he explained, "we haven't made much progress. We'll get there, though."

"I know."

"Jack still hasn't been able to pry any money loose from the banks."

"That doesn't matter any more."

Terry lifted an expressive brow. "What have you been drinking? I want some."

Eden just smiled at him.

They both heard the plane at the same time. Eden went to the doorway and looked out. "It's Jack!" She jumped to the ground and raced down the track.

Jack spotted her as soon as he'd climbed out of the plane and ran toward her as well, catching her in his arms and hugging her tightly to him. "Oh, Eden," he breathed into her hair, "I missed you."

Eden tilted her head back and smiled. She seemed to be doing a lot of that lately. "I missed you, too."

With their arms wrapped around each other, they began the walk to the house. "How did it go with Richard?"

"Easier than I expected. Actually, I think he was relieved."

Jack pulled her closer to his side. "Then he's a fool."

She glanced at his profile as they walked. "Terry told me that you haven't been able to get any money from the banks."

"Not yet."

Eden stopped walking and stood so that she could look directly at him. "I have a confession to make."

"A confession?"

"There was a reason why you couldn't reach me in New York. I was in Spain."

"What were you doing there?"

"Talking with my father."

Jack waited.

Eden was so happy she could hardly contain herself. "You don't need the banks. He opened up the trust fund my grandparents set up for me. There's more than enough money to rebuild the entire station."

Jack just looked at her. "Eden, I told you that I didn't want your money."

"But that was when I didn't have enough to do any good. Now I do. We do."

"I can't take money from you."

Her smile faded away. "Take money from me? But you aren't. I'm investing it in us. In our future."

"Our future, but your money. I know you mean well, Eden, but rebuilding this station is something I have to do on my own."

"Why?"

"Because it's my responsibility."

"And exactly what's my responsibility going to be? Sitting around and looking pretty while our world crumbles around us? Don't you see how absurd this is? I have the wherewithal to make everything all right. I love you and I want to do what I can to help. Please, Jack, let me do this."

Jack, who had had so much on his mind recently, was uncharacteristically insensitive and didn't hear the pleading in Eden's voice. He couldn't see how important his acceptance of what she offered was to her. He took her face in his hands and looked into her eyes. "Eden, ask me anything but this."

She just stood there with a stricken expression on her face.

"I love you," he said quietly.

Eden shook her head as she backed away from him.

"Eden..."

She turned and kept walking until she got to the house. "Terry?" she called as she leaned over the blackened doorsill.

"Yeah?" he yelled from another room.

"Could you come here for a moment?"

He walked out, kneeled down in the doorway and looked at her. "What's up?"

"I hate to ask you this, but could you fly me to Sydney?"

"When?"

"Now."

He looked at Jack, who had followed Eden to the yard and could hear what she was asking. Jack shook his head no.

"Jeez, Eden," he said as he turned his attention back to her. "I wish I could, but there's no way I can make a trip like that for at least a few days."

"I understand. I'll contact one of those charter services."

"I can do that for you. I know all the names." He looked up as Jack walked away towards where the stables had once been. "May I ask what the problem is?"

Eden turned and watched Jack's disappearing back. "Pride," she said quietly.

CHAPTER TEN

AFTER Eden had gone into the kitchen to see Mrs. Cleary, Terry jumped down from the doorway to the ground and walked quickly to the supply shed where Jack was loading things onto a small truck.

"What are you doing?" Terry asked.

"I have to take some supplies out to the men who are watching what's left of the herd."

"Today?"

"They're expecting me."

"What do you want me to do about Eden?"

Jack walked into the shed and back out with an armload of blankets. "Just keep her here until I get back."

"I'll do what I can. What's going on between you two? She was so happy earlier, and now it's as though all the energy has been drained from her."

Jack clenched the muscle in his jaw as he loaded on more supplies. "She wants to give me some kind of trust fund that her grandparents set up for her."

"That's great!"

Jack narrowed his eyes at his brother. "I'm not going to take money from her."

"Why not?" Terry was genuinely confused.

Jack slammed the back of the truck closed. "Look, I just went through this with Eden. I'm not about to stand here and debate it with you. I have to get these things delivered tonight, but I'll be back tomorrow as soon as I can. Keep Eden here until then because she and I have some talking to do. There's no way—no way—I'm going to lose that woman over this."

Terry was silent for a moment as he watched his brother. "Did it ever occur to you that this is about more than money?"

"What are you talking about?"

"You think about it on your long drive." Then Terry, who'd been leaning against the truck, straightened and headed back towards the house.

Jack watched curiously, then climbed into the truck and drove away, leaving a trail of dust behind him.

It was late and Jack was tired. He'd put in another twenty-hour day. As he lay on his blanket staring up at the stars, the last soulful strains of a harmonica drifted through the air. Most of the other men were already asleep, and the few cattle that were left made very little noise.

Eden.

He hadn't been able to get her off his mind all day. He kept remembering images of her: her face covered with soot and sweat as she helped to battle the fire; Eden on her hands and knees, scrubbing the grime in the kitchen; Eden, chasing a calf and bringing it back into the herd and then looking so proud of herself. She was determined to keep up—determined to help.

She should have understood why his pride wouldn't allow him to take her money.

But the expression on her face kept haunting him. Terry was right. There was more to it than the money. But what?

And as suddenly as that, he knew why she'd been willing to leave him over this. After a virtual lifetime of teaching herself not to love and keeping her feelings under strict control, she'd finally met someone in whom she placed her complete trust. She'd come to him yesterday with an open heart, wanting to share herself and all that she had with the man she loved. And Jack had rejected her.

He sat up suddenly and dragged his fingers through his hair. How could he have been so stupid? So utterly blind? She must have felt as though he'd slapped her.

He had to get back to her. Without saying anything to anyone else, he rolled up his blanket and climbed behind the wheel of the truck.

It took him six long hours, driving as fast as conditions would allow, but it wasn't yet dawn when he arrived at the house. Running through the scorched garden, he climbed through the uncovered opening for the front door and into the foyer. Turning on a small lamp sitting on the floor, he went into the living room. The dim light from the foyer shone on Eden as she lay on the floor, her hair spread out around her. She was alone. Jack knelt beside her and just looked for a long time before reaching out to gently touch her cheek.

Eden slowly opened her eyes and looked into his.

"Hello."

"What are you doing here?" she asked as she sat up. "I thought you were spending the night with the stockmen."

"That was my intention. And then I got to thinking."

"About what?"

"You. Me. What we talked about."

Eden didn't say anything.

"I'm sorry."

"Sorry?"

He rubbed his thumb against the smooth line of her jaw. "Eden, I can't believe what I let happen today. I let my pride get between the two of us."

A smile touched her lovely eyes. "Yes, you did."

"I'll never do that again. You and your happiness mean more to me than anything else ever could. Don't ever doubt that."

"So you'll take the money?"

"On one condition."

"What's that?"

"That I repay you as soon as I'm able and that the money go into another trust for our children."

"All right."

Jack pulled her into his arms and held her close. "You weren't really going to leave me, were you?"

"Not for good. I just wanted to go some place where I could think." She looked into his eyes. "I have a hard time doing that when I'm near you."

A tender smile touched his mouth as he pushed her hair away from her face.

"What's so amusing?"

"I was just thinking about the first time I saw you. You were so aloof and untouchable, but I saw the fires that were banked inside you and I wanted to be the one to free them."

"I think that's why I felt so threatened by you. I didn't even know the fires were there until you touched me."

Jack lowered his mouth to hers, and just as he had when they were in that shack, he felt her instant response. It warmed his blood.

"Eden," he said as he raised his head, his voice deep with passion, "we're getting married. Now."

She reached up with a soft hand to touch his face in wonder at what he could make her feel.

He gently caught her hand in his and brought it to his mouth, moving his lips against her palm.

Eden closed her eyes for a moment, the suggestiveness of his gesture affecting her exactly where it was supposed to, then opened them and found her eyes locked with his. A smile touched her mouth and grew. "Now?"

‑ "Now. I'm not spending another night without you."

She loved him so much. "You'll never have to," Eden said softly against his mouth.

EPILOGUE

JACK watched his wife with tender eyes as Eden leaned over their small son and gently pushed his silky hair off his forehead. "Isn't he a miracle?" she asked in wonder.

Jack stood with his arm around her as he gazed into the crib. He wondered if there was ever a child born who was so loved. "Let's go for a walk," he said quietly as he turned off the dimly lit clown lamp.

Eden pulled a light blanket up to her son's shoulders and smoothed her hand over his tiny back before placing a kiss beside his little ear and straightening away from him. Hand in hand, she and Jack walked out onto the rebuilt veranda and through the moonlit garden that Eden had so painstakingly replanted and nurtured into a riot of colour.

Jack suddenly stopped walking and turned Eden into his arms. He gazed at her in the moonlight, his heart in his eyes. "I love you so much."

Eden wound her arms around his neck. "I love you, too."

"Are you happy?"

She gently trailed the tips of her fingers over his cheek. "You know I am."

"I worry sometimes that you might miss the life you had before. Our lives have been filled with such hard work over the past few years."

"And I wouldn't change a moment of it. Look at what we've built together! We've gone from being almost burned out to running a thriving station." She stood on her toes and kissed him lightly on the mouth. "My life was so empty and unfocused before I met you. I don't know how I drifted from year to year like that."

He pulled her closer to him. Her body, with all of the contours his hands knew by heart so well, melted into his. His eyes gazed into hers, and her response to their closeness, never far beneath the surface, flickered gently, warming him.

If someone had told Eden just a few years ago that she could feel this much love for another person, she wouldn't have believed it. And now her greatest fear had been put to rest.

"What are you thinking?" Jack asked.

"About Christopher," she said of their son. "I was so afraid I was going to be like my mother, unable to love a child."

"And now?"

She shook her head. "Oh, Jack." Her eyes filled with tears. "I love him so much it hurts."

Jack smiled and pulled her head onto his shoulder, rubbing his mouth lightly against her fragrant hair. "I know. It's amazing, isn't it? He's amazing. But then, how could he not be? Look at the love that went into his creation.''

Jack reached between them and lifted Eden's face to his. Ever so gently his mouth searched hers, the kiss growing deeper. ''I think we should work on a sister for Chris.''

''Now?'' she asked with a provocative smile.

''Oh, yes,'' he answered softly. ''Right now.''

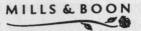

4 FREE
Romances and 2 FREE gifts just for you!

You can enjoy all the heartwarming emotion of true love for FREE! Discover the heartbreak and happiness, the emotion and the tenderness of the modern relationships in Mills & Boon Romances.

We'll send you 4 Romances as a special offer from Mills & Boon Reader Service, along with the opportunity to have 6 captivating new Romances delivered to your door each month.

Claim your FREE books and gifts overleaf...

An irresistible offer from Mills & Boon

Become a regular reader of Romances with Mills & Boon Reader Service and we'll welcome you with 4 books, a CUDDLY TEDDY and a special MYSTERY GIFT all absolutely FREE.

And then look forward to receiving 6 brand new Romances each month, delivered to your door hot off the presses, postage and packing FREE! Plus our free Newsletter featuring author news, competitions, special offers and much more.

This invitation comes with no strings attached. You may cancel or suspend your subscription at any time, and still keep your free books and gifts.

It's so easy. Send no money now. Simply fill in the coupon below and post it to -
Reader Service, FREEPOST, PO Box 236, Croydon, Surrey CR9 9EL.

NO STAMP REQUIRED

Free Books Coupon

Yes! Please rush me 4 FREE Romances and 2 FREE gifts! Please also reserve me a Reader Service subscription. If I decide to subscribe I can look forward to receiving 6 brand new Romances for just £10.80 each month, postage and packing FREE. If I decide not to subscribe I shall write to you within 10 days - I can keep the free books and gifts whatever I choose. I may cancel or suspend my subscription at any time. I am over 18 years of age.

Ms/Mrs/Miss/Mr _____ EP56R

Address _____

_____

Postcode _____ Signature _____

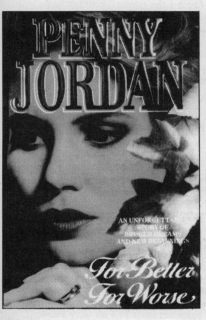

Next Month's Romances

Each month you can choose from a wide variety of romance with Mills & Boon. Below are the new titles to look out for next month, why not ask either Mills & Boon Reader Service or your Newsagent to reserve you a copy of the titles you want to buy – just tick the titles you would like and either post to Reader Service or take it to any Newsagent and ask them to order your books.

Please save me the following titles:	**Please tick**	√
HEART-THROB FOR HIRE	Miranda Lee	
A SECRET REBELLION	Anne Mather	
THE CRUELLEST LIE	Susan Napier	
THE AWAKENED HEART	Betty Neels	
ITALIAN INVADER	Jessica Steele	
A RECKLESS ATTRACTION	Kay Thorpe	
BITTER HONEY	Helen Brooks	
THE POWER OF LOVE	Rosemary Hammond	
MASTER OF DECEIT	Susanne McCarthy	
THE TOUCH OF APHRODITE	Joanna Mansell	
POSSESSED BY LOVE	Natalie Fox	
GOLDEN MISTRESS	Angela Wells	
NOT FOR LOVE	Pamela Hatton	
SHATTERED MIRROR	Kate Walker	
A MOST CONVENIENT MARRIAGE	Suzanne Carey	
TEMPORARY MEASURES	Leigh Michaels	

If you would like to order these books in addition to your regular subscription from Mills & Boon Reader Service please send £1.80 per title to: Mills & Boon Reader Service, Freepost, P.O. Box 236, Croydon, Surrey, CR9 9EL, quote your Subscriber No:................................... (If applicable) and complete the name and address details below. Alternatively, these books are available from many local Newsagents including W.H.Smith, J.Menzies, Martins and other paperback stockists from 11 February 1994.

Name:...

Address:..

....Post Code:........................

To Retailer: If you would like to stock M&B books please contact your regular book/magazine wholesaler for details.

You may be mailed with offers from other reputable companies as a result of this application. If you would rather not take advantage of these opportunities please tick box ☐